GETTING HOME

EARLY WARNING SERIES #2

ANGUS MCLEAN

Published 2020 by Smoking Gun Publications

ISBN 978 0 473 56090 4

ALSO BY ANGUS MCLEAN

Chase Investigations Series

Old Friends

Honey Trap

Sleeping Dogs

Tangled Webs

Dirty Deeds

Red Mist

Fallen Angel

Holy Orders

Deal Breaker

The Division Series

Smoke and Mirrors

Call to Arms

The Shadow Dancers

The Berlin Conspiracy

No Second Chance

Nicki Cooper Mystery Series

The Country Club Caper

Early Warning Series

Martial Law

Getting Home

Stand Fast

GETTING HOME

BY ANGUS MCLEAN

1

The chill of the autumn night was easing now that Curtis was on his second smoke.

The first had been a cigarette, a starter to get the day going, and the second was a point of meth that he shared with his wife, Lena.

The buzz of the P – pure methamphetamine – got his senses pinging and staved off the chill.

He shifted the Beretta semi-auto in his lap, feeling the weight of it. It was a 1301 Tactical in 12-gauge, traded some years back for meth. The extended tubular magazine gave it a 6-round capacity plus one in the chamber, which Curtis always took advantage of.

Lena eyed him as his fingers stroked the receiver and came to rest on the trigger guard.

'You love that fuckin' gun,' she said.

Curtis crooked a smile at her. 'Yes I fuckin' do,' he agreed.

The glint in his eye unnerved Lena. Years ago he had looked at her with desire like that. The only thing he seemed to desire these days was guns and crack.

He saw their niece, Shavaunne, approaching on foot. Behind her was the mouth of a quiet residential cul-de-sac. They were parked in

The Gardens, the "first class" part of Manurewa. He knew the cul-de-sac was quiet because they had been parked in the truck – a red and silver Ford F150 – for the last two hours. Dawn had broken in that time.

Shavaunne and her brother Dice, the big lump of psycho, had been watching a house all night. In that house were a man and a woman, and today they were going to die.

The previous afternoon, the woman had shot and killed Shavaunne's other brother, Jaysin, and his dog, who was only known as Bastard.

Curtis cracked his window as Shavaunne approached.

'Still there,' Shavaunne said without preamble. She was shivering and wiped her nose on the sleeve of her hoody. She looked like she needed a hit.

'Any movement?'

'They're up,' Shavaunne said, eyeing the small glass meth pipe still in Lena's hand. She sniffed the fumes wafting from the truck, desperate for a taste after a night of watching.

'Where's Dice?'

'In the car.'

'He good to go?'

Shavaunne grunted, her eyes on the pipe.

'You deaf, cunt?' Curtis' tone was sharp. 'He good to go?'

'Yeah, fuck, 'course he is. Fuck man, it's cold as shit out here.'

'You want some?' Curtis dug out his tobacco tin, which he always carried. He opened it to show her the gram bag inside and she practically started drooling.

'Yeah, fuck man, I want some. Fuck yeah.'

She reached through the window for it and Curtis gave her the eye. She withdrew her hand quickly. He reached under the car seat and produced a sawn-off over/under shotgun. The butt had been removed to leave just the pistol grip and the twin barrels were no longer than six inches. It was a .410 that he had taken off a dealer.

Shavaunne's eyes gleamed as she took the gun and a handful of spare shells.

'Go cover the back and we'll go in the front,' Curtis said.

Shavaunne nodded and went to step away, but Curtis grabbed her thin wrist. He ignored the anger that flared in her eyes – Shavaunne didn't like being grabbed.

'Remember,' he said, 'they killed your brother.'

She hissed like a cat and jerked her arm away. Curtis turned to Lena.

'Let's go.'

2

Gemma Dobson drained a last pouch of so-called fruit juice and dropped it in the bin. God only knew what was in it, but she needed to stay hydrated and the sugar would give her a boost.

They had some serious walking to do today. Roughly half-way home now, she wanted to get her hands on a car. Do that, and they could be home in under an hour. Bikes would do, but she wasn't counting on that either. More than likely she figured they'd be walking.

The last two days had got them from Freemans Bay in the city here to Manurewa, weathering the gauntlet of gas fires, jammed roads, thugs and cop killers. She had drawn her weapon – a Glock 17 taken from a dead cop – three times and pulled the trigger. One man had died for sure, and she guessed probably another one. It hadn't given her nightmares as such, but she was still processing the fact.

'Good to go?' she said.

Alex nodded and adjusted the straps on his day pack. Two days ago he'd been a colleague she had barely known. Alex Parker from IT, a bespectacled, geeky young guy with dark hair and the complexion of a lab rat. Since then they had travelled together, slept under the stars, looked out for each other.

His mother hadn't made it home yet and he had elected to continue on with Gemma. She felt good about that.

'Come on, let's go for a walk.'

They moved towards the front door and Gemma was about to open it when she caught a flash of movement in her peripheral vision. Hurrying across the neighbour's front lawn onto the driveway was a skinny girl and a massive, hulking man. The girl clutched a pistol of some sort in her hands. They were heading towards the side of the house where she knew they could get around the back.

'Shit.' She saw them disappear from sight and was about to open the door, figuring they could race out the front while the bad guys were at the back, when she saw two more people coming into the driveway. A man carrying a shotgun and a woman beside him. 'Fuck.'

Alex had seen them too and his eyes were popping out of his head. 'Jesus,' he whispered. 'Who're they?'

'Doesn't matter who,' Gemma hissed, already moving. 'We need to get out.'

She'd gone through the house last night, checking their security, and she knew that the pair going round the back had one obstacle in their way. The back fence was six-foot tall and there was a side gate at the back corner. The gate was bolted and padlocked from the inside, due to a burglary some time ago.

The huge man would struggle to get over that, she figured.

They reached the laundry and she checked out the window. Sure enough, the man was battling to heave himself over the gate. The girl was sitting on top of the gate, one leg either side, trying to help him over.

Behind them, the front door rattled. Gemma and Alex looked at each other.

The front door smashed in and they took their cue.

Gemma yanked the back door open, the Glock in her hand, and stepped out. The girl was looking down but the guy saw them and grunted something as Gemma brought the Glock up.

The girl turned, grabbing for her own weapon, and Gemma fired. The girl flinched and lost her balance as the bullet whizzed by her shoulder, and she fell off the gate.

'Go!'

Gemma pushed Alex towards the back fence and followed him as he crushed his mother's flowers and scrambled up the fence. She threw a leg over the top and tumbled over at the same time as the back door crashed open and a shotgun boomed. Splinters showered her as she rolled to her feet in the back garden she'd landed in. Alex was already halfway across the lawn.

Gemma raced after him, heard a thud on the fence behind her and instinctively veered to the right. The shotgun boomed again and a window shattered in the rear of the house as she cut around the side. She made it to the road as Alex sprinted past, white as a ghost.

'They're shooting at us!' he yelped, as if she hadn't noticed.

Gemma ran after him, the day pack bouncing on her back as she ran for her life.

Curtis got to the road, his chest heaving. It was another residential street and there was not a soul in sight.

He scanned in all directions, the barrel of the semi-auto shotgun moving with his gaze. If he saw either of those fuckers, no matter how far away, they were going to cop a load of buckshot.

Shavaunne and Dice reached him, panting and scowling. Curtis glanced past them, seeing Lena still coming.

'You two,' he hissed, 'go find these cunts. You see them, they die. Get it?'

Shavaunne nodded and hurried off to the right, the sawn-off shotgun in her hands. Dice lumbered after her like an ox.

Lena caught up and bent over with her hands on her knees.

'How...the fuck...' she wheezed.

'Too fuckin' slow,' Curtis grated. He looked at her as she spat a thick string of saliva. 'Need to lay off the smokes, babe?'

She raised a middle finger in response.

'Come on, move your fat arse. These fuckers aren't getting away from us again.'

3

The crunch of feet on the gravel driveway announced visitors, but I had already seen them coming.

Rusty and Sophie Van Dijk were a retired couple who lived on a small block across the road. Archie and Jethro, the Border Collie, raced out to meet them. We had eaten already but the oldies were still working through cups of tea and breakfast inside. Rusty ruffled Archie's hair and my son led the older folk up onto the deck where I waited.

'Vee heard the commotion lasht night, Mark,' Rusty said, his Dutch accent still as thick as when he had emigrated years ago. He shook my hand firmly. 'Are you okay?'

I nodded, not quite sure where to start.

'Vee shaw shome of it,' Sophie said. 'Vee shaw you were not hurt, but...shome of them...' She shook her head sadly. 'Bad people.'

I nodded again. 'Two carloads of them,' I said. 'They came with guns and were going to kill us.'

'We stopped them,' Rob said from behind me. He stepped out onto the deck, a steaming cup in his hand. He wore a flannel shirt with the sleeves rolled up and had the Browning High Power holstered on his hip. 'We stopped the bastards before they could hurt us.'

Archie listened with wide eyes, looking at me when he heard his Poppa swear. I motioned for him to go inside but he ignored me. Stubborn like his mother. I ushered him inside and shut the door. He didn't need to hear this conversation.

'How many of dem did you...did you, ahh...' Rusty seemed lost, maybe unsure whether he could even ask.

'Three or four of them,' I said. 'It was dark, so I'm not sure exactly how many.'

Rusty nodded, his face sombre. 'Dis ish no good,' he said. 'Dis shouldn't be happening here in dis country.'

'It remindsh me of shtoriesh from our parentsh,' Sophie agreed. 'Back home during the war, with the Nazish.' She shook her head, her eyes welling up. 'Murdering bashtards,' she muttered.

Rusty put his arm around her shoulders and kissed the top of her head. 'Don't worry, my dear,' he said softly. 'It will be okay. The main thing ish that vee look out for each other, yesh?'

He looked at me when he said it, and I could see the strength behind his eyes. This was a man that meant business. I gave a short nod.

'Exactly,' I said. 'We need to have each other's backs and help each other out.'

'And if those scumbags dare to come back,' Rob said, 'they'll get more of the same.' He nudged me with his elbow. 'Eh, boy?'

I nodded again, not really knowing what to say. Last night I had killed three men, maybe more. Earlier that day I had killed three others. The day before that I had bashed two more with a baseball bat. It hadn't been a normal week.

I looked from Rusty to Sophie to Rob. Three retired folk in their twilight years. They should have been enjoying the quiet life, pottering in the garden and attending club outings and visiting the grandkids. Instead here they were, donkey deep in a national emergency, planning to deal out some lethal justice should anyone come and have another crack at them.

I had no doubt that it wasn't just words. People tend to underestimate older generations, but they forget what these people have been through. These three, and the two inside, were the Baby Boomers who had grown up post-World War Two. They weren't reliant on technology. They didn't expect someone else to do it for them. They had a use for everything and a general knowledge of most things.

I had the feeling they were exactly the sorts of people who would get through a situation like this, and I was pleased to have them around me.

'I think it's best that we make some plans,' I said. 'It's a state of martial law now and I can't see it ending quickly. We're going to have to fend for ourselves for some time.' I opened the door. 'Come in and have a brew.'

4

S weat was pouring off both of them by the time they stopped running and pulled up in a small residential park.

Gemma leaned back against the slide and put her hands on her hips, gasping for breath. For the second time in three days she had jumped more fences than she could remember and run so hard for her life she thought she would either throw up or pass out. She checked her watch. 07:35. She was pretty sure it was only about five minutes since they'd left Alex's house, but it felt like an eternity.

She shrugged her bag off and dug out a water bottle, raising it to her lips.

Alex had collapsed onto the bottom of the slide beside her, lying back on his bag and doing a good impression of a corpse. His shirt front was drenched in sweat. She was impressed that he'd managed to keep going – he was certainly no athlete, but fear obviously worked wonders.

She was about to take a drink when the sound of an approaching vehicle reached them. It was a loud, grunty beast and her immediate reaction was one of dread. She knew who it would be.

'Hide!' She dropped the bottle and left her bag on the ground, scurrying beneath the playground tower which was home to the slide, a fireman's pole and a cargo net. The Glock had jumped into her hand already and she crouched, watching through the slats of the playground. She didn't know where Alex was but didn't dare to call out.

The park was on a main road that ran back towards Manurewa, and the playground was set back from the road, closer to the side street that it backed onto.

Roaring down the road towards them was a red and silver monster of a ute, some kind of American job. Gemma's gut tightened and she knew her instincts had been right. This was them – whoever *they* were – and they were hunting Gemma and Alex like prey.

She gripped the Glock tighter and watched as it slowed. The passenger's window buzzed down and she saw a woman staring out, straight at her. The truck slowed more and she could see a man behind the wheel now, a big man.

Instinct told her that he was the guy with the shotgun, the one who had nearly killed her only minutes ago. She decided then and there that if he came for her again she would shoot the bastard cold dead.

Mark had told her a saying years ago, one he'd been told by a firearms instructor; "Better to be tried by twelve than carried out by six." Meaning it was better to explain your actions to a jury than be dead in a coffin.

Her eyes fell to the black day pack she had left on the ground just a few metres away. It stood out like a Goth at a barn dance, and she was sure the woman must have seen it.

'Gemma?' Alex sounded tense and surprisingly close.

'Quiet.'

'Gemma?'

'*Shush*. They're looking.'

She saw the woman turn and say something to the driver, then the truck began to ease away from the kerb. It picked up speed and disappeared from view.

Gemma let out her breath and came out, grabbing her bag and straightening up. The fallen water bottle was half empty and she quickly drained the rest of it, stuffing it back into her bag in the hopes of refilling it along the way.

Alex emerged from the slide while she drank.

'You know how bloody hard it is not to slide down a slide when you're covered in sweat and wearing a pack?' he said breathlessly. 'I was cramping up.'

'I don't think they saw us,' she replied, putting her bag back on. 'They would've come all guns blazing if they had.'

Alex took the opportunity for a drink as well and she discreetly watched him while she tucked the pistol back into her waistband. It wasn't the most comfortable way to carry it, but it was all she had. Her companion didn't seem as stressed today as she had become used to. Perhaps he felt reconnected with normality having been home. With any luck she would be in the same boat later today.

They got moving again, carefully checking the road for any sign of the red and silver truck before darting across. The playground had been graffitied and Gemma had seen discarded foil wraps under the tower, both things a sure sign that it wasn't a great area. She didn't know who else might be watching them and she had no wish to hang around any longer than they needed to.

'There's a school up ahead,' Alex said, leading the trot down a side street. 'We should be able to refill our bottles.'

Gemma checked over her shoulder for the hundredth time and followed him as he veered off into the grounds of what looked like an intermediate school. They were coming across a playing field and she could see drinking fountains over closer to the buildings and the bike shed.

A bike shed.

'There.' Gemma cut away towards the shed, spotting a handful of bikes in the racks. She was surprised they hadn't been stolen, but hopefully it would work to their advantage.

Alex followed her into the shed, little more than a roof with walls of wire fencing.

'Are they unlocked?' he said, glancing nervously behind them.

'No.' Gemma felt her heart sink. 'They're all bloody locked up. Probably why they haven't been stolen yet.'

'Can you shoot the locks off?'

She cocked an eyebrow at him. 'What, is this a cowboy movie?'

He raised his hands. 'Just an idea. It always seems to work.'

'In the *movies*.'

Gemma turned away and tried to fight back her disappointment. Seeing the bikes had given her a surge of hope and now she could feel herself crashing down again. She cursed and clenched her jaw, staring at the bikes as if willing them to free themselves from their shackles.

Damnit.

'We better keep moving,' Alex said behind her, anxiously watching their backs.

'Hang on...' Gemma continued staring at the bikes, knowing she was looking at something but not seeing it. It took her a moment to click. 'These two...'

She moved over to one rack, which had a blue Avanti men's mountain bike secured to it by a chain through the bike's front wheel. In the adjacent rack was the same model bike in green, only this one was secured through the frame of the bike itself, leaving the front wheel free.

'Do you know much about bikes?' Gemma said.

Alex shrugged. 'I know how to ride them.'

Gemma pointed out the two bikes. 'Take the front wheel off that one and put it on that one. That'll give you a bike. I'll carry on looking.'

His eyes lit up and he set to work.

Gemma soon found a second suitable bike, another Avanti – none of the bikes in the shed were expensive models – in silver. The tyres were pumped and the gears looked to be in good condition. Unfortunately, like all the other bikes present, it was locked properly through the front wheel and the frame.

The lock was sturdy enough that she would need tools she didn't have to open it. She wondered whether she should just follow Alex's suggestion and shoot it off, but the sound of the shot might attract attention. While she crouched there trying to figure out a plan, a memory prodded at her. They had bought her a mountain bike last year, with the intention of doing family bike rides, and she'd got a lock with it.

Mark had been insistent that she change the combination on it before using it.

Factory default setting.

She took the lock in her hands, looking at the four numbers of the combo. She couldn't remember what the factory setting had been on her lock, and it was a different brand to this one, but she knew it was the same digit repeated four times.

The lock in her hands was currently set at 2558. She gave it a tug but it was secure. What were the chances it was still set at the factory default?

Knowing that people were inherently lazy, Gemma figured it was a reasonable guess. It was also a reasonable guess that the owner of the bike hadn't muddled up all the digits when they locked the bike.

She rolled the first and last tumblers around to 5, so the combo read 5555. She gave it a tug and the lock sprung open.

'Crazy,' she muttered to herself. No wonder bikes got stolen all the time.

She left the lock attached to the rack and wheeled the bike over to where Alex was almost finished attaching the front wheel to his new bike. He looked up at her with a grin.

'Looks like we've got wheels,' he said.

5

The house smelled musty and had old lady décor.

'Who are these fucks?' Curtis said, his voice the only sound in the house aside from Dice's heavy breathing.

Curtis looked at the big lump. Whatever was wrong with him had never been formally diagnosed, the Green family not being big on doctors, or anyone else in authority for that matter. Whatever it was, it wasn't good. The boy's mother had done it all while pregnant – booze, drugs, hidings from the old man. The boy had done it all over again once he joined the world, and Curtis knew for a fact that his brother had caused at least one significant head injury to the boy.

All that, plus the Green men were just bad motherfuckers.

He prodded Dice in the chest with a finger the size of a hammer handle.

'Outta shape, boy?'

Dice gave that dumb grin that he had, his buck teeth overshadowing his chin. His dark hair was shaved at the sides and long at the front and back. It was a hell of a mullet.

'Almos' got 'em,' he said. 'Fuck 'em up when I do.'

'Make sure ya fuckin' do,' Curtis growled. He looked past the big lump of psycho to Lena and Shavaunne and beyond them to his two sons, Gunner and Tyson. 'Get searching,' he said. 'We need to know who these people are. We know that, we might know where they'll go next.'

They set to it, ripping open drawers and cupboards and dumping shit everywhere. Curtis stood guard and watched them get into it. He'd been on the receiving end of many raids by the cops over the years, and it felt strange to be on the other side. Usually when he was raiding someone, it was a dealer and blood had already been spilled.

He watched Shavaunne sweep the contents of the kitchen cupboard onto the floor.

It was highly unlikely that the pantry held the clue they were after, but for whatever reason the girl seemed to find it necessary. There was a crash from the bathroom as a wall cabinet was ripped off.

Curtis wondered how long it would take anyone to come and see what was going on. If the neighbours had any sense they'd stay away, and he doubted the cops would be coming. If they did, well, too bad for them. He'd love the chance to mow the pricks down. Any time he'd had a scrap with them before he always came off second best, even if he won the original fight. There was always one who'd come in with a blind shot or a kick in the balls, just to make the point that they were calling the shots, not him.

Well not today. Today was different.

'Here,' Tyson said. He held up a piece of paper from the dining room table. Curtis snatched it from him. It was a hand-written note.

'"Mum, I hope you are safe. I'm okay. I'm going with a work colleague to her house. Her name is Gemma Dobson. I'll wait there with her family until things settle down. I'll be in touch as soon as I can, or come there if you can".' Curtis smirked. 'Got an address here, down around Mercer ways.'

'Guess I know where we're goin' then,' Lena said.

'Makes sense they're not together,' Curtis said. 'She's the one with the gun. What kinda fag would let his woman do the shootin' for him?'

'Gotta be a fuckin' ring-pirate,' Tyson smirked, all staunch bravado. He made a point of shifting the Luger in his waistband and hooked his thumbs in the belt loops of his dirty black jeans.

Curtis mentally rolled his eyes. If the boy was half as smart as he was macho, he'd be a fuckin' genius. At least he could rely on Gunner not to think with his dick.

'Be good to find them before they get all the way down there. Don't wanna waste gas.' Curtis tossed his chin at his two sons. 'You two, Shavaunne and Dice, and me and Mum. Split up in three teams. Go find these pricks. If we don't find 'em by nightfall, we meet up at the barn. Spend the night there and go again tomorrow. Got guns and shit at the barn, so we'll be all good.'

They all knew the barn. An actual barn, it was on a rural property that had no links to the Green family that were known to law enforcement. It had been used for cooking methamphetamine, dishing out punishment beatings and storing stolen gear.

'Want us to use our bikes?' Gunner said. The older of the two boys, he was coming up twenty and was lanky and good with chemicals; he was the brains. Tyson was shorter and heavier and played a lot of video games; he was the muscle.

Curtis gave a nod. 'Be faster. Whatever any of youse do, don't get caught by the pigs. Shoot your way out if ya have to. Everyone got a fire stick?'

He knew they all did but it paid to check. Shavaunne still had the little sawn-off .410. Dice wasn't trusted with a gun, but he always carried a viciously-sharp Crane survival knife like Rambo carried.

Gunner had an old-school-looking Marlin Camp 9 9mm carbine which he loved, sharing the same ammo as the WW2-era Luger pistol his brother carried. Tyson being Tyson, he only had one magazine for his, but Gunner was into gadgets and shit and carried a pouch of spare mags.

Curtis gave them all areas to cover, based on the assumption that their prey would be heading south on foot. He led the way out the door, seeing a nosey neighbour peeking over a fence a few doors down. The head disappeared once they realised they'd been seen.

'Whadda we do with Jays?' Gunner asked.

The younger brother of Shavaunne and Dice had been shot by the woman back up near their home. He had died overnight and his body was laid out in the back seat of Shavaunne's pimped-as-fuck black Nissan Skyline, parked just around the corner.

'Bring him here,' Curtis said, 'and a can of gas. We'll give him a Viking funeral.'

Within a few minutes Jaysin was lying on the couch in the lounge, his arms crossed over his chest and a can of Woodstock bourbon and cola tucked in beside him.

Shavaunne and Dice took a moment to say goodbye, then Curtis turned to his sons.

'Torch it,' he said.

The house was well ablaze when they pulled away. Curtis wasn't bothered by any neighbours seeing them – witnesses had a habit of quickly losing interest where he was concerned. Once shit got back to normal, the cops would have a hard time figuring out how a body with a gunshot wound ended up in some old lady's house.

If things did ever get back to normal.

Right now, Curtis Green didn't give a shit about that. He had revenge on his mind.

6

I scoped out the assembled group as I came down the driveway, recognising a number of neighbours.

They were gathered on the road between our place and the Van Dijks', maybe thirty of them. I saw Bevan standing off to the side with an AR-15 hooked over his shoulder. He was watching and listening, but made it clear he wasn't part of the group.

Rusty and Sophie were in the middle, talking to Brenton and Linda from down the road. I had seen them once since the shit hit the fan, when they had come over and asked to borrow a firearm. I'd given them a sawn-off shotgun I'd taken from a thug, but I didn't see it right now. They had obviously decided – unlike Bevan – that guns didn't need to be part of this conversation. Or maybe they didn't want the other neighbours to know they had one. I guessed I'd find out soon enough.

'Looks kind of official,' Rob muttered beside me. 'This a protest rally or something?'

Heads turned as we reached the end of the drive, and I raised a hand in greeting.

'Morning folks,' I said. 'What's happening?'

There was a shuffling of feet before one man stepped forward. I recognised him as Clyde, a hobby farmer from the next property over. He was a lecturer of some sort and had a big gut and gappy teeth. His wife, Ellette, was tucked in beside him. She was a big woman in a flowery blouse and a long cardigan.

'What happened down here last night?' Clyde said. 'We all heard the shooting and cars coming and going, and I see some blood on the road over there.' He squared his shoulders and puffed his chest out. 'If there's been trouble here, I think we all have a right to know.'

I shrugged. 'No problem. Nobody's hiding anything from you. Some scumbags came here last night to kill us and we fought them off. None of us were hurt, thankfully.'

'And the blood over there?' He jerked a thumb over his shoulder.

'That would probably be where I shot one of them,' I said evenly.

Ellette gasped and put her hand to her mouth. 'Oh my God.'

Another woman in the group put an arm around her shoulders and Ellette folded into her. I managed to not roll my eyes.

'There's more blood up on our driveway and the lawn where my son plays,' I said. 'D'you want to see that too? That would be where two guys with guns were slower than us, and we managed to shoot them before they got inside and killed our family.'

Ellette let out a wail and Clyde gave me a reproachful look. 'Come on man, there's no need to be like that.'

'Like what? Fucked off that some arseholes tried to kill my family? Or fucked off that I'm answering to a kangaroo court about it?' I could feel my cheeks getting hot and my jaw tightened. 'Thanks for your concern, by the way. That's obviously why you've come down here, isn't it? To check on the welfare of your neighbours? Or is to tell me what you think I've done wrong?'

Clyde held up his hands in a placatory manner. 'Look, Mark, of course we're concerned about you and your family. It's just, I understand you had burglars the other night, and you pulled a gun on them?' He turned and looked at Rusty, who frowned. 'Is that right, Rusty? He pulled a gun on a couple of kids?'

'Ish not quite like that,' Rusty said, but Clyde turned back to me.

'So I'm just wondering whether, maybe if you'd handled that

differently, this incident last night might not have happened. That's all.' He spread his hands now, looking round at the assembled group. Playing the politician. 'What d'you think?'

I grit my teeth and glanced at Rob. He had fixed Clyde with a steely glare.

'I killed a man last night,' Rob grated. 'For the first time in my life I had to take a life to save another. It's not something I ever thought I would have to do.'

Clyde opened his mouth to interject but Rob jabbed a gnarly finger at him.

'Shut up,' he said, 'don't you dare interrupt me.' He paused, glaring at Clyde as if challenging him to push his luck. Clyde let out a sigh and stayed silent. 'My wife, my son-in-law, his mother and my grandson, are all in that house.' He gestured towards our home. 'They were getting ready for bed when these bastards came here with guns. Two carloads of them, what, eight people? They came here to this home with only one intention.'

Rob shifted his hard glare across the silent faces before him.

'And I'll be damned if I'm going to let that happen. I didn't live this long and go through all the shit I've been through, to lay down and roll over for pricks like that.' He jabbed a thumb into his chest. 'I served my country. I served *your* country. Anyone else here done that?'

Not a single hand was raised.

'I didn't think so.' Rob stepped back, his piece said.

'Ever been stabbed, Clyde?' I said.

He looked at me quizzically, maybe wondering if I was about to change that for him. I pulled back my sleeve and showed him a small white scar on my left forearm. Others in the group craned to see.

'That's from a screwdriver,' I said. 'I caught a guy breaking into a car and he had a go.'

Clyde looked sceptical. 'It doesn't...'

'Look much?' I said. I shifted my forearm up to cover my face. 'He was going for my head.'

Clyde blinked.

'My point is, you never know what you're coming up against. I saw two guys trying to break into my house. That means they have tools. Tools are weapons. I'd rather pull a gun on them than be stabbed and leave my family defenceless. You do it how you like, but that's how I see things.'

'Someone trespasses on your property,' came another voice, 'they get what's coming to them.'

It was Bevan, still standing off to the side. Clyde looked like he'd sucked on a lemon.

'You can't just go around shooting people for coming on your property,' he said.

'Can't call the cops either,' I said.

'It doesn't mean we have to behave like animals,' Clyde insisted.

I shook my head and considered my words carefully. I wasn't trying to get offside with my neighbours, but I wanted them to at least consider the facts before they jumped to a conclusion. I was getting a little tired of being branded a thug.

'You've heard the news?' I said. 'Martial law's been declared.'

'The military are in the streets now,' Bevan piped up. 'Looters are gunna get shot.'

Clyde made a scoffing noise and looked to his wife, who seemed to have got over her latest bout of dramatics.

'It's true,' I said. I turned my attention from Clyde to the rest of the group, raising my voice so they could all hear. I made eye contact with as many of them as I could while I spoke – this was a message they needed to hear.

'Martial law means that the military are basically in charge now, not the civil authorities. Looters may well be shot. Things are in such shit state that the Government has effectively handed over power to the military.' I paused to let that sink in. 'That means that the Prime Minister has acknowledged she doesn't have the ability to get the country out of the shit and govern properly, at least in the short term.'

'Shoulda done it years ago,' Bevan said.

'This has never happened in this country before,' I said. 'But it has happened overseas. Usually it doesn't go too well. '

'So we can expect the Army to come round and take our guns,' Bevan chipped in.

'Take a breath,' I told him firmly. 'Maybe, maybe not. I'd say it's unlikely, at least right now. With no power on, there're no reliable records of anything, so they won't know who's got guns and who hasn't. I'd expect there to be some pretty bad rioting and looting and general lawlessness for some time, though.'

Clyde's wife burst into another wail and he gave me a reproachful look as he tried to comfort her.

'There's no need to scaremonger, Mark,' he said. 'I think you're overdoing it a little.'

I sighed. I'd had enough. 'I don't think so Clyde, but time will tell. I'll be more than happy if I'm wrong, but until that happens I suggest you don't sit around pontificating and singing Kumbaya. You need to get yourselves sorted for the long haul and keep yourselves safe.'

'What can we do?' someone asked.

'Store water. Plant seeds for vegetables. Use your fuel sparingly. Protect your stock. Use every bit of food, don't waste anything.' I looked around them all. Eyes were wide and faces were sombre. It seemed the message was finally sinking in. 'Look, you all live out here because you have some kind of skills and all of you have some kind of animals. It's time to stop being a hobby farmer and take it seriously. You're a lot better off than most people in the cities.'

'It must be chaos in there,' someone said.

I nodded. 'I'd say so. My wife is in there somewhere, hopefully making her way home.' I felt my gut tighten even as I said the words. *Hopefully.*

There were a few murmurs around the group. I'd said enough and I had stuff to do.

'Take care of yourselves,' I said, 'and look out for each other. It's more important to be a good neighbour now than ever before.'

I stepped away from the group and Rob came with me. As I started up the driveway I glanced over at the Macklin house next door. There had been no activity there the last couple of days and I had no idea where they were. The Macklin family owned a good-sized farm but weren't hands-on farmers, preferring to let others do the dirty work for them.

Bevan had access to their place and I'd seen him over there recently.

Bevan.

I turned and spotted him still lurking on the fringes of the group. He caught my eye and I looked pointedly over at the Macklin house, then back at him. He gave me nothing back and sifted away from the group, moving back down the road towards his own place. His AR-15 was still slung over his shoulder and he wore camo pants under his khaki jacket.

Something about him unnerved me.

7

T he mood in the community centre was angry and Henry Roimata was struggling to keep a lid on it.

He hadn't slept since getting home last night, they'd had the dead to deal with, and he'd had a shitload of explaining to do. The missus, the families of the boys who'd been killed – even though some of them had been on the raid anyway – and everyone else who wanted a piece of the fuckin' action.

They were all gathered now, mid-morning, and the air was getting thick with smoke – tobacco, dope and crack. No one gave a shit anymore. Two days down and no one gave a shit.

Not that anyone in the Roimata family had ever given much of a shit. With pockets of the family spread all over South Auckland and North Waikato, barely a job between them, it was a constant procession of Roimatas to the various jails around the country. At one stage Henry had been just down the road in Spring Hill with two of his brothers, one son and four cousins.

Spring Hill was still locked down for now, but it was only a matter of time before the screws were forced to open the gates and let the inmates out. Henry knew they would only have enough food for maybe one more day. When those gates opened, his family numbers would swell again. Manukau was home to a men's prison, a women's prison and a youth justice secure facility. They would open up too and the area would be flooded with more hardened criminals than ever before.

'You gunna fuckin' get on with it, Henry?' The voice belonged to Jake, the next youngest Roimata brother. He was the only one that Henry would ever let talk to him like that, but he gave him a scowl all the same.

'Yep.' Henry pushed up from his folding chair on the stage of the community centre and walked slowly to the front. A hush began to fall over the residents of Meremere and they waited for him to speak.

Henry waited until they were all quiet, concentrating hard on getting it right. He got it right, he'd be all good. Get it wrong and he was fucked.

He'd seen people do this shit on TV before, preachers and politicians and the like. They stood up there lookin' all statesman-like, serious and contemplative, like a lot was runnin' through their head and they were workin' through the options. It inspired confidence in their people, made them realise just how smart the big kahuna was, why they needed him so bad.

Henry tried to channel that up on stage, even subconsciously sucked in his gut. Off to the side, Jake rolled his eyes and wished his big brother would get the fuck on with it and stop playin' with his dick. He hadn't spent a day travelling down here from Pukekohe – where he'd been tending to two of his boys who got fucked up by some arsehole cop with a baseball bat – to listen to Henry pretending he was Winston fuckin' Peters.

'Last night...catastrophe struck our *whanau* (family),' Henry started. 'We went to speak to a man who had assaulted two of our *mokopuna* (children), to set things right. He was a violent man and we lost some of our brothers to his hand.'

There were angry murmurings among the crowd. Jake watched them, sussing out who the angry ones were, the rabble-rousers.

'We barely made it out alive, I have to say,' Henry said. 'I feel lucky to be here today, speaking to you.' He put his hand to his chest and looked to the sky as if the gods were looking down on him. 'The last bullet fired by that man...missed my own head by a millimetre. I looked in his eyes and I knew he was gonna kill me, right there and then.' He gave a full-body shudder and shook his head. 'I felt the heat of the bullet as it went by. I tell you, *whanau*, if I hadn't moved at the last split-second, I'd be dead too.'

Jake suppressed a grunt of derision. He'd heard a different version, but it was typical of Henry to talk it up.

'Fuck him!' someone shouted from the crowd. 'That cunt needs to fuckin' die!'

Henry held out his hands to calm the rising agreement. 'I agree, brother, I agree. He brought harm to our *whanau*, and we will strike back ten-fold. That motherfucker is gonna pay for his sins with blood.'

Jake raised his eyebrows in surprise. This was more like it. This he could work with.

'We will take the fight back to this *pakeha* (white European) invader, we will reclaim our *mana* (pride) and our land, and we will avenge the deaths of our brothers.'

The crowd cheered as one, fists pumping and feet stomping on the wooden floor. Henry rode the wave, his chest swelling with pride, and even Jake cracked a grin.

'But we need to be smart.' The crowd shushed again, hoping this wasn't going to be some kind of chicken-shit approach to gaining their revenge. 'We need weapons to do this properly, and we need weapons to defend ourselves. I guarantee you one thing.' Henry raised his hand in the air, one finger pointing skyward. 'I guarantee you one thing...the *pakeha* will resort to their old ways of killing the indigenous people and taking our land. They did it before, and they will do it again!'

The crowd cheered again, angry now, knowing his words to be the truth. They all knew the history.

In the front row of the crowd, an old lady frowned and chewed on her gums. She was listening and hearing, if not quite comprehending it. It was not what she wanted to hear.

'They will take the opportunity of a lawless state to violate our rights and disregard the treaty! *Te tiroti o Waitangi* (the treaty of Waitangi), which guarantees us certain rights as the indigenous people of *Aotearoa* (New Zealand), will mean nothing. And we won't stand for it.'

Henry half-turned towards his brother, and Jake gave a quizzical frown.

'My brother here, he has access to what we need. He can get us what we need, so that we are ready for what's coming.'

Jake felt a kick of adrenaline. As a patched member of the Bandits gang, he had access alright. *Fuck yeah*; now his brother was talkin'.

Shit was about to get real.

The old lady turned and weaved her way through the crowd. She needed some fresh air.

8

The wind felt good on Gemma's face as she got some downhill momentum, easing off the pedals for a bit and letting gravity do its thing.

Alex was beside her, gripping the handlebars for dear life. She wondered if there was any kind of physical activity that he was comfortable with. But for all his lack of experience, he was constantly surprising her.

In only two days he'd gone from being just an IT geek from work who asked if he could tag along with her on the way home, to being her constant companion. He'd foraged for supplies, he'd saved her from a beating, he'd been beside her when she literally fought for their lives.

'All good, Alex?' she called out.

He glanced over his shoulder at her with a smile, but the smile quickly faded as eh looked past her. 'Don't know.'

Gemma wobbled as she looked behind her, scanning the street they'd just raced down. The school was only a few hundred metres back and their bike journey had barely begun.

'Oh shit.'

Two dirt bikes, haring across the school field on a beeline towards them. She didn't know who was on them but she knew it was trouble.

'Go for it!' Alex shouted, pumping his knees hard and hunching low over the handlebars. Gemma followed suit but she knew there was no way they could outrun the dirt bikes. She could hear them now, the high tinny whine of their engines getting closer.

'Down here!' Gemma swerved hard right into a side street, spotting a playground in a park a hundred metres further down.

Alex came after her, perilously close to losing it before he got his balance and pedalled hard. A shot rang out behind them, then another.

'Keep going!' Gemma panted. 'The alley!'

They hit the footpath and were into the park, racing towards the alleyway on the other side. It was partially blocked by a concrete bollard to stop cars going down it, and it gave Gemma a flash of an idea. She went first, crashing into the tin side wall of the alley before pushing off and away.

The whine of the dirt bikes was close now, but she could hear that they'd split up. Good move on their part; bad for her and Alex.

She came out the other end of the alleyway, cut left and skidded to a halt. Alex did the same, looking at her in confusion.

'Whaddayadoin'? he gasped, his eyes wide.

'Grab this.'

Gemma yanked the tow rope from her bag and thrust one end of it at him. She darted across the mouth of the alley, ducking down beside the side wall as the first dirt bike arrived at the far end. Alex realised what she was doing and gave a nod, gripping the loose rope in both hands.

The bike raced down the alley, the engine echoing loudly in the narrow passage, and all too soon it was on them.

Gemma jerked her end of the rope up to chest height, Alex was a split-second slower, and the rider collected it at an angle across his chest. His bike kept going and he hung in the air for a moment before hitting the pavement on his back. His skull impacted with a sickening wet smack.

The bike lost momentum, wobbled and tipped over with the engine still running.

Gemma started pulling in the rope, transfixed by the sight of the rider on the ground. His mouth was moving but no sound was coming out. His limbs were twitching. He was a solidly built young guy with dark hair.

'Jesus,' Alex said.

The sound of the second bike bore down on them and they saw it racing around the corner into the short cul-de-sac they'd come to. The rider gunned it towards them.

Alex legged it into the property next door and Gemma dropped the rope and raced straight back up the alleyway. Her bag was bouncing on her back and she was struggling to get her arm out of the straps.

When they'd started off on the bikes she'd moved the Glock into her bag, because it was too uncomfortable in her waistband and she was scared it would fall out. It was a decision she was bitterly regretting as she wrestled with her bag and also tried to get out of the alleyway.

She reached the park and ducked off to the right, yanking the strap off her shoulder and scrabbling with the top opening. *One more second.*

The impact of a boot in her side was like getting hit by a cement mixer, and it threw her sideways to the ground. The bike hit the deck and the rider was there before she could even try to get up. She took another boot to the ribs, flipping her over again, and she caught a glimpse of a tall, lanky young guy over her as she tried to get to her knees.

'You fuckin' bitch,' he was screaming. A third boot to the side. 'You fuckin' cunt-whore, you fuckin' killed my little brother...' A stomp to the shoulder knocked her flat. 'You fuckin' slut, I'll fuck you up you cunt.'

Gemma wheezed, unable to get any air into her lungs, her fingers digging into the dirt, her eyes watering. This was it. He was going to kill her.

Gunner slammed his boot into her hip, flipping her onto her side and exposing her front. He aimed a kick at her face but she moved at the last moment, so instead of taking her head off it just opened up a cut on her cheekbone.

The sky was above her. Clouds, puffy and white, a bit of grey. The dirt bike engine had died. All Gemma could hear was her own wheezing and the blood pounding in her head. She was in agony and she knew she couldn't beat this guy. She couldn't even get up.

Gunner kicked her hard in the gut, causing her knees to fold up belatedly to protect her. She wretched like she was going to vomit.

He cocked his leg again and Gemma saw it coming. This was it. He was about to kill her and there was nothing she could do to stop it. *Fuck him, I won't give up.* She dug her fingers into the dirt and gave it everything, pushing herself up.

She didn't hear the hollow thump as a fence paling smashed into Gunner's back, but she took the full impact of him collapsing across her and knocking her flat again. She felt the follow-up hits to his torso as Alex hit him again and again, and she heard his groaning in her ear.

Then his weight was gone and Alex was helping her up to her knees.

'Are you alive?' he was asking. 'Jesus Christ that was brutal, I thought he was going to kill you.'

'Urrggghhh.' Gemma did her best to get air into her lungs but it felt like her own body was fighting her every step of the way. 'Unnhhhh.'

She stayed on all fours for a long time, drooling onto the grass as she tried to get herself working properly. Everywhere hurt. It felt like she had broken ribs and she could feel her cheek puffing up.

'We need to get going,' Alex was saying somewhere in the distance. 'There's people around.'

Gemma held onto him while she eased herself to her feet. He poured water on her face and gave her a drink. She looked down at the guy who'd beaten her. He was lying prone, not moving.

'Is he...dead?' She put her hands on her hips and took a full breath. She arched her back and heard a joint crack, then another. 'Ahh, shit.'

'I don't know.' Alex went over and nudged him with a foot. The guy didn't move. 'I hit him pretty hard.'

'Good.' Gemma wiped her face. 'Thanks.'

She staggered over to her bag, got the Glock out, and shoved it in her waistband. From now on she wouldn't be without it. She looked at the young guy again then at his dirt bike. 'He's got a gun.'

She undid the bungy cord that held the Marlin carbine to his handlebars, and took the gun.

'We need to go, Gemma. There might be others.'

'Take that belt off him.' She pointed to the camo-pattern bum bag he wore, bearing several pouches. 'Must be ammo.'

Alex rolled the guy onto his back, recoiling when he saw the blood coming from his mouth. The guy was unconscious but his chest was rising and falling. He quickly undid the belt and passed it to Gemma, who secured it around her own waist. The guy was lean enough to be a near-enough size for her.

She took another few moments to find the safety and the magazine release on the carbine – it was not too different to Mark's little .22 rifle. The magazine held a dozen rounds, and the pouches held four more magazines and two boxes of 9mm ammunition, the same calibre as the Glock. She realised what a great find it was, to not only get a second weapon but also spare ammo in the same calibre. It went some way to alleviating the pain from the beating the prick had given her.

'D'you know how to ride a motorbike?' she asked.

Alex shook his head.

'Bummer. Me neither.'

'I'll get our bikes.'

While he did so, Gemma caught her breath and looked down at the lanky young guy.

'You fuckin' prick,' she muttered, feeling a sudden surge of anger.

She stepped in and have him a hard kick to the ribs. The movement caused a sharp pain through her own side and she gasped, gingerly touching her ribs. She looked up to see Alex arriving with the bikes, watching her.

'Feel better?' he said.

'A little. Let's go.'

9

T he gully to the northern side of our house formed the boundary with the neighbouring property where Clyde and Ellette lived.

A creek ran through it and we liked to look for frogs down there. The creek was deep enough to be home to eels, and we had built a dam there over summer, creating a rock pool which Archie and Jethro had played in.

Standing at the top of the gully now, I planned out my move. I saw the gully as potentially a strength or a weakness if we got attacked. A strength if we used it for cover, or a weakness if the enemy – whoever they were – used it as an access point to our property. The land actually belonged to us, so I could do what I wanted with it.

My mind flicked back to who "the enemy" might be. The crew from Meremere, coming back for revenge? Some other unknown pillagers? Neighbours looking for food?

It was an open field but I was determined to make it hard for whoever came.

My last trip to Mitre 10 Mega on the day this all went down had been to load up the trailer with building supplies and bits and pieces I had thought I might need. One such item had been barbed wire.

Wearing heavy duty working gloves, I lugged a reel of barbed wire to the end of the gully furthest from the road and skirted to the far side. I was in the trees and scrub there with Clyde's boundary fence just in front of me.

I could see their house across the paddock, and both of them were in the yard, tending to their garden. Their kids were adults and living away from home, so I was pretty sure it was just the two of them living there.

If an intruder came across the paddock and climbed the fence to enter the gully, they had to contend with branches and scrub that made the job harder. Their attention was likely to be on getting their footing sorted at that stage, so their eyes would probably be down.

I dropped the reel of barbed wire where it was and took another reel from the builder's apron round my waist. I tied one end to a branch at shoulder height and worked my way along the treeline, winding the line around branches at irregular intervals.

It was a lightweight fishing line with a small hook every six inches or so. After tying it off at the far end I came back to the barbed wire and moved into the trees a couple of metres. I hooked that up at thigh level all the way through the trees, weaving it between the under-growth to best conceal it. If someone got over the fence and didn't lose an eye on the fishing line, with any luck they would rip their leg open on the barbed wire.

I snipped the wire and secured it then cut back through the gully towards my own place. There was more that I wanted to do in that area, because I saw it as the biggest risk to us, but I also needed to make sure that we were safe back at the house.

The shed attached to the garage was destined to become a sleepout in due course, but I hadn't got around to it just yet. That was about to change.

Rob was already at work in there, with the door and windows open for ventilation. It was big enough for a double bedroom and had a smaller room off it which would be the bathroom.

Rob had moved all the boxed crap that we'd stored in there through the internal door into the garage, working up a sweat as he did so. He stopped to take a drink and wipe his brow as I entered the room.

'What've you got in there,' he said, 'boxes of bloody bricks?'

'Who knows?' I said. 'It's mostly Gemma's old stuff.'

'Better not bin any of it then,' he said with a knowing smile.

We swept the room out and set to work proper. The walls were uninsulated, which we would need to address in time if the room was to be used as a bedroom, but right now I had other plans for it.

The high roof gave a vantage point to spot any intruders, and there were vents at each end. Birds nested there and dropped their crap down the side of the shed. I used the long ladder from the garage and clambered up to the attic, balancing on the beams so I didn't put a foot through the ceiling.

Rob passed up several fence palings and I nailed them in place across the joists, forming a safe walkway from end to end, using the hatch as the centre point. I cleared out the bird nests from each vent, shoving the straw and twigs and rubbish down between the slats to fall to the ground below. There was a clear view out towards the road at one end and down to the back of our property at the other.

I scanned each way, working out arcs and points of interest. Ideally we would have decked out our advantage point with a proper sniper rifle with a suppressor, a good scope and night vision capability, but we didn't have that. It would likely be Rob up here with his bolt action Lee Enfield. Old school.

He was a decent shot on the iron sights and he had sufficient ammo, unless an actual army invaded, and it was a good role for him to fill in our defences. I didn't want him running around down below, jumping fences and burrowing in the dirt. That was my job.

Coming back down the ladder, I found that Archie and Jethro had come to investigate. The dog was sprawled in the doorway with one eye open, and Archie was helping his Poppa set a sheet of plywood against one wall.

'What's this for, Poppa?' he said. He leaned against the sheet with both hands, holding it steady while Rob got the cordless drill set up.

'Just a bit of insulation,' Rob said easily. 'Hold it steady.'

He buzzed in the first screw and moved down to Archie's end, setting another screw on the bit. He let it bite then released the pressure and offered the drill to Archie.

'Here sunshine, you want to finish it?'

Archie concentrated and gripped the drill with both hands, and drove the screw in. From there he was away, helping Rob to secure the sheet and move onto the next one. The ply would provide some insulation from the weather, but the main purpose was to provide some level of protection if we got fired on. Short of steel plating, it was the best we had right now.

Rob attached a couple of hooks to the wall above the side window and drilled corresponding holes in another sheet of ply, giving us the capability to cover the window securely.

Lunchtime was approaching, and it reminded me to bring some food and water into the sleepout, just in case.

Sandy called us in for lunch and the five of us sat on the deck and ate together. With the power being off and on, we had cleaned out the fridge and were almost finished the fresh food. The chilly bins of ice were nearly melted now but were still cold enough to keep milk, butter and the like chilled.

We ate sandwiches and fruit and drank tea, and Archie chatted away about a project he'd been working on at school, filling in anyone who would listen about the intricacies of making a dinosaur out of air-dried clay.

He didn't seem terribly bothered yet by the recent events, but I was waiting for it to take hold. I knew he was worried about Gemma, and sure enough, he brought it up again.

'Dad, when d'you think Mum'll get home?' He was in the chair beside me at the outside table, swinging his legs and munching on a cheese and jam sandwich.

I took a swallow of tea. 'Not sure bud. Hopefully soon though, eh?' I gave him a conspiratorial grin. 'You know she doesn't trust the boys to keep the house in order, does she?'

He laughed, his eyes sparkling with mischief. 'Na, 'cause the boys always make a mess and the place smells like farts and feet.' He glanced at Grandma, feigning innocence. 'What, Grandma? That's what she says!'

My mother, Jenny, reached over and ruffled his hair. 'You're quite a trick, young Archie.'

I started clearing the plates away but my mother stopped me, taking them from me.

'You carry on doing what you need to do,' she said. 'I'll tidy these up.'

'Thanks.' I gave her a smile. 'What's for dinner?'

She frowned and fussed with the plates as I followed her inside. 'Oh, I don't know what she's organising.' *She* being Sandy, the other grandmother and therefore the competition

I suppressed a groan. I had enough on my hands without the old matriarchs butting heads.

I headed back to work, building an external layer of protection around the sleepout. I had tree stumps and logs, a pile of dirty old bricks and pavers, and feed sacks I could fill with dirt as makeshift sandbags. There were a few old oil drums around the back of the implements shed which would make a great chicane in the driveway once they were filled with dirt.

I had a lot to do but I knew it had to be done. There was one goal, and one goal only – keep my family safe. If we were attacked again, we would be ready to stand fast.

10

Gemma's body was aching and she was finding it hard to take full breaths.

They had left the two brothers behind them and pedalled as fast as they could to clear the area, sticking to the main road south towards Takanini. Her attacker's rifle was slung across Alex's back and he also carried a bum-bag of spare magazines for it. A pair of military helicopters had flown low overhead not long after their run-in with the bogun brothers, but the soldiers on board had paid them no mind.

She wondered if the two young guys were dead. She figured the one who had been clotheslined probably was, but maybe not the other one. She doubted that Alex had hit him hard enough, and she wondered if she would have. If she'd had the chance to while he was beating her, she knew she would have killed him. He would have left her no choice, because simply giving up wasn't an option.

They were passing a new development of houses now and she could see plenty more activity than she'd seen earlier. Vehicles were moving about and people were coming and going from houses. Smoke was spiralling skywards from a few blocks over, the dense black smoke that came from a house fire.

Outside one house she saw a man and woman arguing while the baby in her arms screamed, a huddle of thugs outside another were sharing a bong. The man belted the woman across the face then stormed off inside, slamming the front door hard enough for the glass pane to shatter. The woman cried and the baby continued to scream.

The thugs blew puffs of foul smoke and chuckled at something one of them said. One of them, a fat guy with a wispy goatee and a gold medallion over a basketball top, watched Gemma and Alex cycle past. He grabbed his crotch and said something she didn't hear, but it made his mates laugh.

They kept going, seeing an intersection with dead traffic lights coming up. An Army Land Rover was parked in the middle of the intersection and a squad of soldiers were fanned out around it, facing in all direction and openly carrying rifles.

Gemma braked, calling out to Alex. 'Stop, stop.'

He circled back to her and came alongside. 'What is it?'

'We can't go past the soldiers with our guns.'

He gave her a double-take. 'They wouldn't shoot us, would they?'

'Why wouldn't they?' She put a hand to her side and pressed down, breathing through the pain.

'We're normal people.' Alex looked aghast at the very idea.

'They don't know that. They'll just see people with guns.'

'I don't...' He shook his head and looked away. 'This is just...crazy.'

Gemma straightened her back and took shallow breaths. 'You're right,' she wheezed. 'Jesus that hurts...'

'I mean...this isn't normal.' Alex gestured around them. Further up the road the group of thugs were still puffing away and the smell carried on the wind to them. Alex waved in their general direction. 'They're smoking drugs in the street, y'know? What's up with that?'

'Stop waving your arms,' Gemma told him. 'You're drawing attention to us.'

'And you're all banged up, and I just beat a guy to a pulp with a piece of frickin' wood, and we got shot at, and...'

'Alex.' Gemma's tone was sharp. 'Shut up. Just shut up.'

He stopped talking and looked past her. 'Uh-oh,' he said.

Gemma could feel some of the tightness easing ever so slightly. She was pretty sure there'd be some kind of painkillers in the first aid kit – if she could just unsling her bag without popping a rib.

'Gemma,' Alex said.

She paused, catching the edge in his voice. Looking past him, she saw the soldiers facing their way shifting, looking more alert now and focussing behind her.

'I think we need to get moving,' Alex said with urgency, starting to turn his bike towards the soldiers.

Gemma turned and looked behind her. The group of thugs who had smoking weed outside their house had moved out into the road, and had been joined by several more unsavoury types. Two of them had pitbulls on chains and at least three of them were carrying lengths of timber. They were eyeing up the soldiers two hundred yards away. A fat young woman came out from a nearby yard, lugging a bucket with both hands. She staggered to the kerb and some of the group joined her, taking garden stones from the bucket.

'Let's go,' Gemma agreed. She glanced around them, realising they were smack-bang in the middle of the soldiers and thugs. 'Over there.'

She gestured towards a side lane that ran off the main road. It went into the housing area, but at least it would take them out of the firing line. The soldiers had readied their weapons and their body language screamed readiness. In the other direction, the larger group of thugs, emboldened by their drugs and street bravado, were fanning out across the road and calling out to the soldiers.

''sup, G? One-out?'

'Fuckin' faggots, come down here and play.'

Alex led the way into the side lane as the abuse started flying behind them, followed closely by the first stones being hurled. Gemma noted, to their credit, that the soldiers remained stoic. She wondered how long that would last.

They followed the side lane in a loop out to a road where they could see the soldiers another hundred yards or so down to their right.

'Keep going.' Gemma pedalled across the road and into another side street, keen to leave the growing scene behind them. The side street was empty and ran roughly south, so they stuck to it for now.

As she pedalled though, Gemma knew she needed to get some medical help pretty soon, or she'd be in serious trouble.

11

The haze of meth smoke was thick in the kitchen of Henry Roimata's house. The small table was filled by Henry, Jake, Henry's best buddy Tintz and Jake's fellow Bandit, Little Dog.

All were large men with tattooed arms and faces that bore the scars of hard living. Little Dog was a particularly nasty looking man, with missing teeth, boob tats beside both eyes – from back when each tear drop represented a full year inside, not a month – and a stamp across his throat that read FUCK THE WORLD. His position in the Bandits was that of Sergeant-at-Arms, the enforcer of the gang. Like many Bandits he was a 501, a deportee from Australia so-named after Section 501 of the Immigration Act which allowed the Aussies to send foreign-born criminals or other undesirables back to their birth nations.

It had been the single biggest change to the criminal scene in New Zealand in decades, introducing a large number of hardened career criminals to a country most of them had never known, a place they had no roots, no family support and no desire to be. It was a situation that had allowed real gangs, the worst of the worst, to flourish.

Little Dog and Jake were shining examples of the Government's inability to front up and deal with the problem head-on.

'So you can?' Henry said, exhaling a lungful of smoke slowly.

Little Dog nodded, shifting his gaze to Jake. 'Yeah.'

'How soon?'

Little Dog chewed his tongue for a long moment. 'Day, two.'

Henry nodded eagerly. That was good. 'And what can you get?'

Little Dog eyed him coolly. He didn't have much time for Jake's brother, but business was business. 'Whaddaya need? I can get M4s, Sigs, Steyrs. Prob'ly some grenades. Maybe a Minimi.'

Henry nodded again, buzzing now. This was the shit. 'Fuck yeah,' he said. 'Whatever you got, bro. Sounds good.' He narrowed his eyes now, assuming his best poker face. 'An' what's the terms of the deal?'

Little Dog almost laughed. What the fuck was the clown trying to play cool for now? He was on the hook already, as barred up as a virgin on his wedding night. Little Dog was pretty sure he could've asked for twenty a piece and got it. He bit back his laughter and shrugged.

'See if I can get what you want, eh? Work it out then, bro.'

Henry gave a sage nod, glancing quickly at Tintz beside him. Tintz hadn't said a word since the meeting began, just sat there, him and his black wraparounds and his bad breath. Tintz might have looked back at Henry, or he might've been asleep.

'Sounds good, bro. We can work it out.' He reached across the table and shook hands with Little Dog.

Chair legs scraped on the lino floor as Little Dog pushed back and stood. 'Be in touch,' he said.

He walked outside, the fresh air hitting him. He sucked it in. He liked a smoke as much as the next man, but these cunts smoked too much. He walked down the unpaved driveway from Henry's shitbox old house to the road, where two of his boys waited.

Henry was a fuckin' clown, but Little Dog was okay to deal with him. If the deal didn't come through, Little Dog would just stand over the cunt anyway and take what he had. Jake would understand; it wasn't like he hadn't done worse back in Oz. Jake would be cool with it.

As for that homo who wore sharkies all the time, day and night? That fag was lookin' for a hiding. His time would come.

Pua and Dion straightened up when Little Dog reached them. Samoan brothers, they were maxed out on the 'roids, both fuckin' huge units.

'All good, LD?' Pua said. He had the butt of a pistol sticking out of his waistband.

'Uh.' Little Dog grunted and cracked the passenger door of the white Range Rover. 'Go.'

Dion got behind the wheel, Pua in the back. A Steyr AUG was laid across the back seat.

'Gonna Willie's?' Dion said. His voice was surprisingly soft for such a big unit.

'Yeah.' Little Dog slid on his shades, gold-rimmed Rayban aviators. 'Got bidness to do.'

12

As soon as the Range Rover disappeared, Henry pushed back his own chair and stood.

'Come on,' he said. 'Get the boys together. Gotta job for them.'

Jake and Tintz followed him out the back and over the low wire mesh fence to the grounds of the community hall. A bunch of the young fellas were lounging around there, smoking and talking smack like usual. With the phones being down they'd had to go old school, so a portable CD player was vibrating to some Bones, Thugs and Harmony. At least they appreciated the classics.

'Eh.' Jake gave them a jerk of his head, signalling them to get up.

Jake carried a lot of weight around these ways and the boys all scrambled to their feet, eager to listen – all aside from a chunky kid known as Fester. His cheeks were so pudgy that he looked like one of those dogs with a mashed-up face. He forced himself to his feet, leaning heavily on his knees as he got up.

'When you're fuckin' ready,' Jake growled.

The right thing to do would have been to apologise and get the lead out. Fester did neither, just lumbered over to join the group, saying nothing. Jake took one step forward and punched him square in the face. As Fester fell backwards, Jake caught him by the shirtfront and lowered him to the ground, continuing to punch him in the face and head until he hit the deck.

The rest of the boys watched in silence, no one willing to step in. No one fronted up to Jake Roimata.

Fester stayed down, nursing his bloodied face and trying to catch his breath. Jake stepped back and looked at the rest of the boys. He flexed his fingers and breathed through his nose, pumped up now.

'Anybody else wanna fuck with me?'

Nobody said a word.

Henry stepped up now, game face on.

'I gotta job for you boys,' he said. 'That honky motherfucker that shot us up...we gonna get him. We're getting some guns, fuckin' military hardware, and we're gonna go up to his place and blow his shit away. Him, his family, whatever. We're gonna fuck them up. Yeah?'

There were enthusiastic nods, just as he had known there would be. Young gangster wannabes were always eager to please.

'But first we're gonna go and have a recce, suss it out in daylight.' Henry caught Jake's surprised look and ignored it. 'We need to have a proper look at it so when we go back we know where the fuck we're goin' and we fuck him up proper, eh?'

More nods of enthusiasm, a few nervous glances between the boys.

'I need six of you to come with me.'

Nine hands shot up straight away and he chuckled. He picked the boys he wanted, the ones he knew could handle themselves, and moved them over to the side. The other three shuffled their feet and stared at the ground.

'You three gotta special job to do here,' Henry told them. 'You gotta help Jake and Tintz look after this place, make sure no arsehole sneaks behind our back when we're not looking, eh? Jake gotta couple guns you can use while you on patrol here, eh?'

They looked more hopeful now, happy they weren't missing out completely.

'You six, over to my place. Move it.'

They hustled to the fence and Jake came alongside Henry.

'What're you doin'? he hissed, keeping his voice low so the others wouldn't hear.

Henry eyed him. 'This motherfucker is goin' down, little brother. He fucked us over the first time but he ain't doin' it again.'

'Why not wait until dark?'

''cause we can't see in the fuckin' dark.'

'Little Dog could get us some of that night vision shit.' Jake's tone was frustrated now. 'It's too dangerous to go in the daytime, he'll see you coming and you know he's prepared to fight. This ain't like robbin' some fuckin' Indian dairy.'

Henry squared around face to face with his younger brother. 'Don't you fuckin' question me, boy,' he grated. 'This is how we're fuckin' doin' it, eh? We go have a look, help me plan it. We get the good shit from Little Dog, we go back and we blow his ass away. Get it?'

Jake opened his mouth to argue but the look in his brother's eye stopped him. He knew there was no arguing when Henry was like this. He sucked down a breath, stepped back, and gave a short nod.

'Okay,' he said. 'I'll get some guns.'

13

B evan was having a coffee and a smoke when he saw the man stop outside his house. He took a last drag on the rollie and snibbed it out, tucking the butt into the pocket of his camouflage jacket. Tobacco was bound to get scarce in days to come.

The man hesitated outside, looking up the short driveway towards the white weatherboard farmhouse. Having second thoughts, maybe.

Bevan knocked back the dregs of his coffee, set the mug down on the step beside him, and stood. The man saw him, paused some more then raised a hand in greeting. Bevan nodded back.

He didn't get many visitors, probably on account of most people finding him strange. Socially awkward, even. He didn't give a shit. Sarge raised his big head beside him and looked at the man who was now slowly approaching. Didn't growl, not yet anyway. Being a fifty kilo German shepherd, usually a look was enough to make people think twice.

'Afternoon, Bevan.'

'Brenton.'

The visitor stopped a few metres away as if still unsure, like the last few metres meant he hadn't really committed yet.

'Does he bite?' Brenton asked, warily watching Sarge. Sarge stared back at him, his ears pricked, but stayed lying down.

'Yep.' Bevan gave a small smile. 'Mostly only other dogs though.'

Brenton smiled weakly and kept his hands in his pockets. He looked around and shifted his feet awkwardly.

'What can I do for you, Brenton?'

'I...ahh...I got a shotgun,' he said, unsure where to start.

'Good for you. So have I.'

Brenton let out a nervous laugh, but Bevan didn't smile. It was simply a fact.

'I don't have much ammunition for it though, and I was wondering if maybe...um, maybe I could...buy some off you?'

Bevan looked at him. They were about the same size – although Bevan had the soft frame of an office worker, not an outdoorsman – both in their mid-thirties, both had brown hair. But they were worlds apart.

'Your money's not much good to me right now,' he said, and Brenton's face fell.

'Oh, okay, I just thought...sorry.'

Bevan shook his head. 'Look, don't worry. We can barter. What animals have you got?'

Brenton looked surprised. 'Um, half a dozen chooks. A cat.'

Bevan cocked an eyebrow. 'That's it?'

Brenton nodded, embarrassed.

'Okay...you got a vege garden?'

Brenton nodded, more confident now. 'For sure. Linda's a good gardener.'

'Good. We can trade then. You got something I want.'

The look of relief on Brenton's face almost made Bevan smile. These fuckin' city boys were stressed and needed to get out more.

'You got a 12-gauge?'

'Yes.'

'Right, I'll swap you a box of birdshot – that's twenty rounds – for access to your vege garden for a fortnight. You got broccoli?'

'Yep.'

'Potatoes?'

'No.'

'Peas?'

'Yep.'

Bevan nodded. 'Done. Wait here.' He ducked inside and returned a minute later with a box of ammo. 'Nice doing business with you.'

Brenton tucked the box into his pocket. 'I guess it's like Mark said, we've all gotta look out for each other at the moment.'

Bevan gave a grunt. 'He did say that. Me, I tend to rely on myself. Any thieving shitheads come round here and they'll know all about it.'

He sat down on the step again and watched Brenton head back down the drive. He was a jittery fucker, Bevan decided. Not somebody he'd want to rely on when the shit hit the fan. Mark was a different story. Bevan was pretty sure the man didn't like him, but it didn't mean Bevan couldn't appreciate a kindred soul when he saw one. Mark was a man he would feel comfortable beside in a fight. Problem was, he was about the only one around there.

Bevan began rolling himself a smoke and was licking the paper when he heard running feet. Brenton was racing down the drive towards him, a panicked look on his face.

'Bevan! They're back!'

Sarge watched him coming, ears forward, ready for action.

'Who?'

'The...the guys...the shitheads...' Brenton got to him, panting and pointing down towards the corner. 'Down there...two cars of them...I saw one...one's got a gun.'

Bevan was on his feet in a flash, grabbing the AR-15 from inside the door. He slipped his arm through the sling and snatched a second weapon from just inside the front door.

'Ever fired one before?'

'No.' Brenton looked at the gun that Bevan handed him.

'It's a Benelli M2 Super 90. Semi-auto 12-gauge. It's loaded, five in the tube and one up the spout.' Bevan rattled the specs off like a salesman in a hurry. He flicked off the AR-15's safety and headed down the driveway. 'Come on, let's get these fuckers.'

14

'Someone's coming.'

Henry lowered the binoculars he'd been using to scope out the target's address, and looked at the three figures approaching down the road. Two men and a dog. The men both carried weapons in their hands.

'Is that him?' he wondered out loud, but he hadn't clearly seen the face of the man the previous night.

The first guy, who appeared to be the leader, had an assault rifle and wore a camo jacket. The guy slightly behind him, who looked less certain of himself, wore a polar fleece and jeans.

It could be either of them, but Henry would have put his money on the first guy. They were about seventy metres away now.

'Wanna party, eh?' Henry glanced over his shoulder at the six young guys with him. One of them had a bolt action 7mm hunting rifle, another a .22 pea-shooter, the other a long-barrelled shotgun that had been used for clay bird shooting before it was stolen. 'Gimme that rifle.'

He took the rifle and flicked off the safety, settling the butt into his shoulder. The two men were closer to fifty yards away now.

'Throw down your weapons,' the first guy shouted at them, his rifle up in the aim. 'Hands in the air!'

Henry stayed behind the beaten-up Subaru, leaning across the roof. He took aim at the first guy.

'Throw down your weapons or I'll shoot!' the first guy bellowed.

'Homo.' Henry squeezed the trigger, hearing a hollow click. The young fella had been carrying an empty chamber. 'Fuck's sake.'

Henry worked the bolt, hearing the first guy shout, 'Gun!'

Two shots rang out and Henry got the rifle back in the aim, seeing movement across his sights as he pulled the trigger.

Bevan fired a double tap and jinked to his left, hearing the boom of a rifle and a grunt from Brenton behind him.

He got down to one knee, AR-15 up, pumping the trigger towards the gunman. There was a shitty-looking Subaru and a white Toyota station wagon parked on the shoulder just at the corner, almost out of sight. He couldn't tell how many bad guys there were, but it looked to be eight or ten.

He put half a dozen rounds into the two cars, adrenaline coursing through him, then was up and moving to the ditch at the side of the road. He saw a bullet ping off the road ahead of him, well wide, and heard the boom of a shotgun from somewhere. Good, Brenton was in the fight. Maybe he wasn't such a fuckin' pansy after all.

Bevan got to the ditch, Sarge leaping in beside him, and got himself up against the side, nice and low with the rifle over the lip. He squeezed off another couple of rounds, un-aimed, to keep the pricks' heads down.

The rifle and a shotgun boomed and Bevan heard the impact of rounds hitting the dirt near him. He looked over his shoulder for Brenton, hoping he'd thought to take cover.

His heart sank when he saw his neighbour sprawled on the road, not moving.

15

As soon as the gunfire erupted, I was moving, running to the house and getting everyone from inside.

I got them low and we ran to the sleepout, where Rob was waiting with his rifle. I shut them inside and told them to stay put until I got back. I had to find out what was going on. There were wide eyes all around and Archie was getting upset, not wanting me to go, but I gave him a grin I didn't feel and a squeeze and backed out the door.

Knowing the activity was at the end of the road, I cut through the paddock into the Macklins' property and across their front paddock. Their house stood still and silent and I wondered again where they were.

Working my way closer to the road, I could see now that there was a body lying in the road. Someone was in the ditch across the road and a bit further up, firing what sounded like a .223 semi-auto – I guessed that was Bevan with his AR-15.

Up at the corner several people were gathered around two cars, at least three of them shooting back towards the guy in the ditch. It was like the bloody Wild West and I was the sheriff coming to the rescue.

I checked my gear, making sure I was ready, and pulled a small pair of 8x20 binos from a pouch on my belt.

I zeroed in on the body on the road first, and immediately recognised Brenton. He wasn't moving and there was a shotgun lying near him. I confirmed that it was Bevan in the ditch, popping up to rip off a volley of shots before ducking down again. He could have done with moving because the other guys had his location nailed and it was only a matter of time before someone got lucky.

The guys shooting at him had no tactical nous, and were wandering about freely, trying to see their target. I could hear the crack of a hunting rifle, the boom of a shotgun and the light pop of a .22.

One was leaning across the bonnet of the Subaru that had come visiting previously, and as he worked the bolt of his rifle, I recognised the leader that I'd spoken to. I'd told him not to come back or I would kill them.

He hadn't listened, and it was time to put my money where my mouth was. If these guys overran Bevan, they would keep coming. They had come armed and looking for a fight. Any time for negotiation, if there had been one, was long gone.

I put the binos away, crawled under the side fence into the next paddock and worked my way towards the road. I got into a corner where I had thick fence posts for some cover, blackberries in the roadside ditch for a bit of concealment, and a better angle.

I was about seventy metres away from the guys at the cars. The .357 Magnum was a good pistol round but a bit light for longer shots, but in the absence of anything better I would have to make do.

Bevan was still ripping off shots, the odd one hitting one of the cars, but he was pretty much firing blind.

I focussed on the leader first, tucking in behind the fence posts and using them as a shooting platform. Nice and steady. The crosshairs of the 3-9x scope settled on his left ribs, clearly visible from my angle, and I gently squeezed through the trigger pull.

The rifle jutted against my shoulder and the guy dropped from view.

I worked the lever, keeping in the aim, and spotted the guy with the shotgun. He was hurrying around the back of the car, coming into my view now, eager to see what had happened to his mate.

I sighted on his chest, breathed and squeezed, and he moved at the last nano-second. Instead of drilling through his chest, the round took him in the left shoulder, spinning him like a top. He went down out of sight but I could hear him screaming.

Bevan leaped up and gave it the full Rambo, spraying rounds from the hip as fast as he could pull the trigger. Glass punched out of the car windows and a wing mirror went flying, but it was a lot of noise for little result. He ducked back down again and someone popped up with the shotgun, letting off a blast in Bevan's general direction.

I sent a round his way, narrowly missing him as he ducked down behind the car.

The next thing I heard was the revving of the station wagon and it took off in a cloud of dirt and dust, leaving two guys scrambling to get in the Subaru. I saw them piling one of the wounded into the back and one of them had one of the guns in his free hand. I could just see him through a side window, so I got the best angle I could and pumped a round through the window. Glass went everywhere and I followed it with another shot, hoping for a lucky hit.

The Subaru got going and took off down the road.

I stayed where I was, feeding fresh rounds into the tube of the Rossi. I waited for maybe half a minute before rising cautiously and calling out to Bevan.

'That you, Mark?' He popped out of the ditch with a crazy grin on his face, clearly high on adrenaline and gun smoke. His dog was wandering about looking confused.

My own system was firing on all cylinders from the massive adrenaline dump and my ears were ringing like hell. I joined him on the road and we went over to Brenton. I nearly jumped out of my skin when his arm moved, and I realised he was alive.

Lying on his side, he was breathing shallowly and bleeding from a wound of some sort to his chest. The front of his jacket looked wet.

He raised his eyes to us and groaned, gently putting a hand to his chest.

'Can't...breathe,' he whispered.

I knelt beside him and checked his wound. I pulled open his jacket and was surprised at the lack of blood. He was clearly in pain though, and I could see an impact on his chest that was bleeding, rather than a puncture wound.

The shotgun lay off to the side and I could see that the sling was half off it. The steel buckle on the sling was twisted and damaged.

I checked his back and found no exit wound.

'You're the luckiest fucker alive,' I told him. 'The bullet hit the buckle on your sling.'

Brenton looked confused and Bevan let out a whooping laugh.

'Is he okay?' Rob arrived behind me, the Lee Enfield in his hands.

I nodded. 'Probably sore as hell, but I don't think it's actually gone in. Might have a broken rib or something though.'

He looked at me. 'What about you?'

'I'm fine.'

'Same guys?'

'Yup.'

'Did you get them?'

'Shot two with guns, one was the head honcho from last night. Maybe a third. Don't know if they're dead or just wounded, they all took off.'

Rob nodded and looked over at Bevan, who was checking his magazines. 'What about you, John Wayne? Did ya hit anyone?'

'Pretty sure I got at least one,' he said. I was pretty sure he hadn't, but it didn't matter right now.

'I'm going to clear down there,' I said. 'See if they left anything behind.'

'I'll come with you,' Rob said.

We checked around the area where the bad guys had been, finding a few cigarette butts and several spent casings in 7mm, .22 and 12-gauge.

'Three shooters,' Rob mused, casting a wary eye around.

'This is crazy,' I said. 'It's gotta stop.'

'They don't get it, do they?'

'No, they do not.' I set my jaw. 'Enough's enough; I'm not having these pricks keep coming back.'

'What're you going to do?' Rob said cautiously.

'This is our home, Rob. It's time to take the fight to them.'

His brow creased and he chewed his lip. 'And how do you plan on explaining that to the ladies? And the wee fella?'

I looked him in the eye. 'It needs to be done, Rob. You know it as well as I do. We are not gunna live in fear of these pricks.'

He stared at me a long time before slowly beginning to nod. 'I understand,' he said.

'We going after them?' Bevan interrupted. Seeing my face, he gave a fist pump then went for a high five. I ignored it so he pumped his fist again instead. '*Yes*. Let me get my shit.'

Rob and I looked at each other. Brenton had sat up now and I could see Linda approaching down the road, Rusty and Sophie not far behind.

'Best you get going then,' Rob said. 'But watch your back.'

I turned to go and he grabbed me roughly by the arm, pulling me into an unexpected hug. I clapped him on the back.

'Come home,' he rasped.

16

Gemma and Alex had managed to get from Takanini to Papakura before she called a halt. Her ribs were screaming and the exertion was making it almost impossible to breathe.

They had got through a residential area and were on the edge of the town centre now. The railway lines to their left were empty and there was hardly any traffic on the road. People were still walking about and they noticed as they got closer to town that the people they passed were getting rougher and more boisterous. They saw broken windows and damage in almost every building and smoke was drifting across the rooftops, adding to the smell wafting south from the city.

Passing one side street, they had stones and bottles thrown at them by a group of youths who yelled abuse and tried to give chase. Leaving them behind and getting around a corner, Gemma gave a shout and pulled up.

Alex wheeled back to her, looking over her shoulder for any sign of the yobs. They were nowhere to be seen, but he could see that his companion was in trouble. She was holding her ribs and wheezing, and sweat was running down her face.

'I need...stop,' she huffed.

Alex glanced around for somewhere to take cover, spotting a block of commercial premises just ahead at the northern end of the town centre. 'Come on.'

He led the way and they went round the back into a service alley. The rear doors were all secure, most of them with heavy steel security doors. He settled on a plain wooden door which was the rear entrance to a travel agency. He took the small pry bar from Gemma's bag and levered the door open while she leaned against the wall and kept watch.

After bringing their bikes inside, Alex secured the door again as best he could, placing a table against it. He found Gemma in the kitchenette, rummaging through the fridge. The milk had curdled and the fridge smelled off, but the small freezer compartment wasn't completely defrosted yet.

'Here.' Gemma passed him a bowl she had found. 'Put ice...in that.'

Alex found a butter knife and chipped cubes out of an ice tray into the bowl. She handed him a tea towel and he followed her into a rear office, away from the main entrance. She dropped her bag and awkwardly tried to remove her poly-prop top and T-shirt.

'Help.'

Gemma was no exhibitionist, but her medical needs outweighed her modesty just now. If Alex was turned on by a dirty, sweaty woman who'd worn the same clothes for three days and looked like she'd been battered to hell, then she'd just have to shoot him. He clumsily helped her and she sat in her bra while he wrapped ice cubes in the tea towel.

Her ribs were heavily bruised and scraped, and she gasped when he placed the ice pack on her skin. She took it from him and held it against the sorest part, clenching her teeth and sucking up the pain.

'Jesus,' Alex muttered. 'That looks pretty painful.'

Gemma let out a short laugh. 'You're...a man. I...squeezed out...a baby.'

'Why're you laughing?' Alex felt himself smiling. 'That's ridiculous; you should be crying.'

'I laugh...when it...hurts...a lot.'

'Did you laugh when you had your baby?'

She nodded, shifting the ice pack to another spot. 'Mark said...it was...the weird...weirdest thing.'

Alex chuckled. He took a drink of water then rummaged in his bag and came out with some of the first aid gear they had acquired.

'Got some Panadol,' he said. 'I'll see if I can find something better.'

While he went off, Gemma focussed on her injuries. Now that she had the chance to sit and rest and ice her ribs, she was fairly sure there was nothing broken. The ice should help reduce the swelling, which would make it easier to breathe. She dug a Snickers bar out of her bag and munched while she sat, wondering what Mark and Archie were doing right at that moment.

Alex came back with a big grin on his face and two new items in his hand.

'Look what I found. Voltaren anti-inflammatories and some arnica cream.'

'Good man.' Gemma took two of the tablets from him and washed them down. The tea towel was soaked now and she put it aside. She pulled her tops back on, moving a bit freer now with a torso that felt like a frozen side of beef.

They sat for a few minutes, drinking and eating. Gemma was almost dozing off when Alex suddenly blurted out, 'My boyfriend dumped me.'

She looked at him curiously. 'Well, that's pretty shit.'

'He dumped me a week ago and I had to move back in with my Mum. We'd been planning a holiday to the Philippines, and he suddenly decides that he's "lost his spark".' Alex made the quotation marks with his fingers and pulled a face. 'Son of a bitch.' He shook his head and gave a chuckle. 'Actually, that's not fair. His Mum's really nice.'

Gemma smiled and drained her bottle. 'What's his name?'

'Jeremy.'

'Well, Jeremy can get fucked,' Gemma said emphatically, and he laughed. 'He doesn't know what he's missing out on.'

'Yeah, fuck you Jeremy.' Alex gave a double bird at the ceiling. 'Your loss.'

'Why the Philippines?' Gemma said. 'That's an unusual holiday destination.'

'He's part-Filipino. I was going to meet all the family.'

'I'm sorry.' Gemma didn't know what else to say. She barely knew Alex anyway.

Alex looked around at their surroundings and sighed. 'I guess it doesn't really matter now, does it?'

Seeing he was getting into a funk, Gemma changed the subject.

'Thanks for looking after me,' she said. 'Things weren't going so well there.'

'Huh. That guy gave you a hell of a hiding.' His brow furrowed. 'I think he would've killed you.'

Gemma gave an involuntary shudder. 'I think so too. Lucky you were there to save the day, eh?'

Alex pulled a face, clasping his hands together. 'I was shitting myself. I've never hit anyone like that before.'

'Well I'm bloody glad you did.' Gemma smiled reassuringly. 'You saved my arse.' Her eye fell to the rifle they had taken from her attacker. 'Pass me that, please?'

She sat back in the chair and looked the weapon over. It was marked as a Marlin Model 9 Camp Carbine, and reminded her of Mark's little .22 rifle with its wooden stock and short magazine. She found the safety and made sure it was on. She found the magazine release and dropped the mag, then worked the bolt and popped the round from the chamber.

Checking the base of the brass, she saw it was a 9mm Luger round, the same as the Glock. She double-checked it against the Glock ammo to be sure, realising what a stroke of luck they'd had. Having just one calibre for two weapons had to make it easier.

She fed the round back into the magazine and pressed down with her thumb, confirming the mag was full. She counted twelve rounds, reloaded the carbine and worked the bolt to chamber a round.

She felt Alex's eyes on her and looked up.

'How did you know to do all that?' he said.

Gemma shrugged self-consciously. 'Mark has guns at home, and I've shot them a little bit. This is very similar to one of them, but a different calibre. It's pretty basic.'

Alex gave a snort. 'Not to me it's not. Unless it's got a motherboard or a mouse, I'm lost with technical stuff.'

'It's not technical at all. Here.' Gemma handed the carbine to him and he gingerly took it. 'It won't bite, just keep your finger off the trigger.'

She spent the next ten minutes running him through how to use the weapon, feeling like an expert with her own limited knowledge against his complete lack. She got him to unload it fully, work the bolt, take aim with the iron sights and dry fire it several times. She could see he still wasn't entirely comfortable with it, but the more he handled the weapon the more he seemed to relax, just as she had when Mark had first taken her out.

The camo-pattern nylon bum-bag that the owner had carried contained six spare magazines for the Marlin, and Gemma checked that they were all loaded and fit the weapon. Satisfied, she handed the bum-bag to Alex.

'You better wear that too,' she said. 'You carry the rifle and I'll keep the pistol.'

He looked hesitant, but took the bag. 'Okay...'

'We both need to be able to defend ourselves,' Gemma said firmly. 'The more prepared we are, the more likely we are to get home.'

17

T he ute was a real farm workhorse, a rugged Toyota Hilux single cab with grass and crap in the footwell and dirty windows.

Not surprising, given the way that Bevan threw it about. We were almost at the motorway onramp at Mercer when I told him to ease up. He pulled to the shoulder of the road and looked at me expectantly.

'What?'

'We need to get our shit together,' I said. 'We can't just chase these pricks into town, not knowing what we're going into, without being prepared.'

I climbed out and adjusted my belt. The Ruger was holstered on my hip, I had plenty of spare ammo in the pouches and the Rossi was ready to go. Before we left his place, Bevan had raced back inside and grabbed more gear.

God only knew what kind of an arsenal he had in there, but in addition to his own AR-15 and the Benelli shotgun he'd recovered from Brenton, he'd brought a bandolier that looked like it came from the Vietnam war, the pouches loaded with 30-round AR-15 magazines.

I checked my weapons and ammo, ensuring I had everything close to hand.

He was doing the same with his belt pouches, replacing his spent mags, and I had the feeling he was in his element. It unsettled me that he'd been living just down the road all this time, with an armoury of some sort in his house and what seemed like an unhealthy obsession with firearms, and I'd had no idea.

Right now, as long as he stayed straight and on my side, we were all good.

Bevan chucked the ute in gear and we got moving.

The highway onramp was clear but the highway itself was dotted with abandoned vehicles and scattered debris. A burned-out people-mover was slewed across the overbridge. I wondered what had happened to the people I'd seen fighting down on the highway last time I'd crossed that bridge.

Bevan weaved his way past the abandoned vehicles and a few minutes later we were turning off onto Island Block Road. A quick right took us onto Te Puea Ave and up a hill parallel to the highway. Te Puea Ave was the main drag of Meremere, a small town of roughly half a dozen roads. I knew the school was on the left and the lone shop, library and community hall on the right.

We crested the hill and immediately saw the two cars we'd been following parked outside the community hall. Several people, mostly blokes, were gathered outside the hall. I could see two bodies laid down near the vehicles and it was clear that they'd just arrived back to an emotional homecoming.

Heads turned as we approached and I saw a guy step behind the Subaru and reach inside.

Bevan pulled up and I bailed out with the Rossi up in the shoulder, safety off and trained on the guy reaching into the car. I moved towards him at a fast walk, heel-toe, heel-toe, eyes scanning but keeping a focus on the guy I identified as a threat.

The rest of them seemed stunned, unsure of how to react.

'Get your fuckin' hands up! Hands up!'

I was about ten metres away and could see him clearly now.

Looking through the remaining windows of the Subaru, I could see that he had his hands on the barrel of a rifle but the weapon was still leaning against the front seat.

He locked eyes with me and stopped moving, but he didn't let go of the weapon.

'Put it down or I will fuckin' shoot you, shitbird,' I told him. 'Don't try me.'

His eyes narrowed and I could almost see the cogs turning in his head, assessing me and calculating his move. I knew that if we lost this first interaction, we would lose everything. The first pad of my index finger was on the trigger, gently cupping it, and I applied the first pressure.

The guy at the car was a bee's dick away from being toast, and the realisation suddenly seemed to click.

He lifted his hands away from the rifle and stepped back, raising both hands to shoulder height. I felt myself breathe and I eased off the trigger, but I kept the weapon up and crab-walked around to my left, keeping the whole group in view.

'All good, Bevan?'

'Yep.'

'Who the fuck you think you are?' one of the guys shouted. 'Come here pointing guns at us like we're dogs?'

'You the guys who fuckin' murdered our *whanau*?' someone else said.

'These two?' I said, gesturing at the two bodies with my barrel. 'Tell me where they were killed.'

Nobody said anything aside from a few muttered curses.

'If they're two of the pricks that came to our place and started shooting, then yeah, we killed them.'

More muttered curses then the guy who'd gone for the weapon stepped forward and spat, eyeing me all the time.

'Fuck youse,' he said. 'You cunts are dead.'

'And there's your fuckin' problem,' I said. I lowered the Rossi Puma slightly and eyeballed him. He was average height but solidly built, with scars showing through his crew cut hair and tough stamps on most of his visible skin. 'We're not. We're here because you thieving fucks keep coming to us. Stop coming and you'll stop getting shot. It's pretty fuckin' simple.'

More people were coming out of the community hall, curious about what was going on. Nobody seemed overly concerned that we were armed.

'You arseholes just come out shooting,' one of the young guys piped up. He had blood on his shirt front and his arms, and I guessed he'd been one of the guys who'd been there. 'We didn't have a fuckin' chance. We're tryin' to get away and youse just shot us in our backs, ow.'

'The only dudes I shot were shooting back at us,' I said firmly. 'So knock that bullshit off.'

I saw an elderly Maori woman coming forward from the hall, scuffs on her feet and a tea towel in her hands. She paused to look down at the two bodies, shook her head and whispered something, then came towards me.

The guy who'd gone for the rifle was still trying to staunch me out, arms out like he was carrying basketballs, huffing and puffing and eyeballing me. I'd had about enough of his shit.

'You're a fuckin' coward,' he spat. 'Gonna fuck you up, you fuckin' white-bread shit.'

'Any day, motherfucker,' I told him.

The old lady shushed him and patted his arm as she went past him, and he lowered his eyes, stepping aside. She stopped a metre short of me and I lowered my weapon. Up close I could see she was probably knocking eighty, had few teeth left in her head, and a face with more lines than a Motley Crue party in 1986.

She was a good foot shorter than me and she craned her head to look at me, studying my face for a few long moments.

'Is it true?' she said. 'You killed these boys?'

I nodded. 'Yeah, we did.'

She nodded slowly. 'And they come to your house first? You say they're stealing?'

'Yeah, they came with firearms. They shot first and we defended ourselves.'

The old lady nodded again. I could see sadness in her face but also resilience. There were many stories behind those old brown eyes.

'Were any of your people hurt?'

'One. But he should survive.'

She nodded some more. 'I'm sorry,' she said. 'I'm sorry this has happened.'

'So am I,' I said. 'I understand you'll be hurting, but trust me, these guys brought the fight to us. We're just trying to get by the best we can, the same as everyone. If we came here to your village and were started shooting and stealing, I'd expect you to defend yourselves as well.'

'True, true.' More nodding. 'There will be no more. No more. You go now, and let us do our thing, okay?'

'Yep, fair enough.' I nodded and extended my hand.

She shook it with a surprisingly hard grip and pulled me in closer. 'But don't come back, my friend. This is our village; not the place for you. Some of our young ones, they...can be hot-headed.' She nodded to herself. 'My name is Aroha. I'm the nan to most of these boys. Hot-headed, some of them...and they will be angry.'

I held her grip. She was giving me a message but I had my own to deliver too.

'I understand that, and I appreciate your honesty. Your young ones also need to get it into their heads that we will not back down. We're not looking for a fight, but I guarantee you, if they come to us, they will lose.' I looked her in the eye. 'Okay?'

The old lady nodded and gave a slight smile. The resilience was showing through now.

'We understand each other,' she said quietly.

We stepped back from each other and I glanced over to Bevan. He was off to my side using the ute as cover, still watching the crowd.

'One more thing before we go,' I called out, directing myself towards the head honcho who'd been staunching me. 'Hand over the guns you used against us today.'

'Fuck off,' the head honcho retorted.

'Don't be silly about it. You've got two options,' I said. 'Either give them up voluntarily, or we come and take them.'

The old lady said something to him. The guy didn't like it and he tried to argue, but she cut him off and pointed him towards the car. He gestured at one of the minions, who carefully removed the rifle and carried it towards me like it was radio-active, his eyes flitting constantly to my weapon.

'Put it in the back of the truck,' I told him. I turned back towards the head honcho again. 'And the others? I counted at least three.'

He shrugged arrogantly. ''at's all we got. Musta lost them on the way or something.'

I decided to cut my losses, and backed over to the ute. I covered Bevan while he got behind the wheel then I climbed in beside him, keeping the group covered through the open window.

'Better not see you again,' I said to the head honcho as we started to move. He spat and gave me the bird and we drove away.

JAKE ROIMATA WATCHED the two men in the ute go, his nerves jangling and his rage barely contained.

'See you again, motherfucker,' he muttered. 'You a dead man.'

He turned and stalked inside the hall, already formulating a plan.

18

T hey had watched the ute leave with the two guys in it.

They seemed like the main guys, both having assault rifles and being the ones who had done all the shooting.

Once the ute was gone the guy who was wounded had been helped up and made his way back down the road with a woman they presumed was his wife.

The old man had put the dog back in the yard of the closest house then headed back down the road too. They watched him turn into the driveway at the house they had been watching earlier with Henry and the others. He went inside. Both of the boys breathed a sigh of relief at that point. Even though the dude was old, he carried a rifle and he looked like he knew how to use it.

Cyrus had been on the raid last night and was pretty sure the old man had killed one of the boys. His companion and best friend, Donald, had lost his brother to these men. When Henry and TK got hit, Cyrus and Donald had taken cover in the ditch, Donald still carrying the bolt action Norinco .22 Jake had given them earlier. The other two guns had gone in the cars with the others – the chicken-shits had fucked off as soon as people started going down.

Cyrus wasn't sure if he was brave or stupid, but he knew Donald was spoiling for revenge and he knew they had a job to do. It was supposed to have just been a recce but Henry had fucked that up when he started shooting, not that he would ever say that out loud. You didn't say shit like that about Henry Roimata unless you wanted your arse kicked. Things had changed now, and Cyrus was smart enough to recognise an opportunity when he saw one.

The only way they could get any revenge for their brothers now was to strike when the enemy were weak. From what he had heard them say, they were going after the crew back to Meremere. The main guy – Henry reckoned he was a cop – had missed him and Donald hiding in the ditch across the road when he'd come and checked after the shootout. Donald had wanted to blow him away then and there but Cyrus had resisted, knowing they would just get blown away themselves by the others.

Better to take their time and do it right.

They rose from the ditch now, both filthy dirty from the mud and shit at the bottom of it, but both also pumped because they had a plan.

Cyrus led the way, cutting across the road and into the paddock on the other side. He was no country boy but he had done a Limited Service Volunteer course a year back. His case worker at WINZ, who'd been trying to get him into a job since he left school and home at fifteen, had put him forward.

Cyrus hadn't enjoyed it – all cops and social workers and shit trying to be your friend and make you interested in being a soldier. Cyrus had no interest in being a soldier – he was after his Bandits patch and that was that. He lasted two weeks on LSV before he got caught smoking crack and was kicked out.

Donald was sixteen, a lean, hard boy who played league and liked to fight. He'd spent most of the last year in juvie for armed robberies, and he was heading for the big house if he went down on his current charges. It was him and his younger brother who had first tried to break into this place the other night, somehow picking the wrong fuckin' house first up that night after burgling six others the night before.

They made their way through the paddocks, past the big flash house to the hedgerow that they knew was the boundary of their target house. They paused at the hedgerow and Cyrus looked at Donald, who was still holding the Norinco. It was a cheap Chinese rifle but it would do the job.

'All goods, bro?'

'Yeah, all goods.'

'Get in, shoot whoever we see, take whatever we see, jack one o' their sleds and get gone, eh?'

'Fuck yeah, bro.' Donald pushed his way under the hedgerow, sliding the rifle ahead of him.

19

Jenny Dobson had been furious to learn that Mark had gone off chasing the guys they'd been shooting at, and Rob couldn't really blame her.

He wasn't so happy about it himself, but he did understand the reason why. Besides, Mark was bull-headed and wouldn't have changed his mind anyway. Not that that had done anything to calm Jenny down, and now she and Sandy were thrashing it out in the lounge, Sandy doing her best to calm the woman down and keep her on track, Jenny venting at the whole damn world and her thick-headed son in particular.

Archie was watching it all with wide eyes, old enough and smart enough to know that Grandma was pissed off with his Dad, but not quite knowing why. He'd heard the shooting and had stayed inside with the women while Poppa went out to help, and he knew that his Dad and the neighbour Bevan had fought with some bad guys.

Rob caught his eye and gestured for him to follow, leading him into the kitchen and away from the tense conversation.

'Grandma's really annoyed with Dad, Poppa,' Archie said, hoisting himself up onto the bench. 'She said he's got a thick head. That's not very nice, is it?'

Rob resisted the urge to draw a comparison to Jenny herself, instead smiling politely and agreeing with his grandson. 'I think she's pretty annoyed right now,' he said, 'but she'll calm down. Adults are like that, young Archie.'

'When will Dad be back?'

'Shouldn't be far away. D'you want to help me get dinner ready?'

'It's not dinner time yet, Poppa. We haven't even had afternoon tea yet.'

'I know, but we need to get ready for it. We've got chicken and rice, and we better have some veges too, I suppose.'

'Can we have beans and carrots?'

Rob poked him in the ribs with a finger. 'You still don't like peas, eh?'

'Na, gross. But I like beans and carrots though.'

'Here.' Rob handed him a bowl of food scraps. 'Go chuck that to the pig, will you? Then you can help me peel some carrots.'

The boy hopped down and took the bowl of scraps out, and Rob shook his head to himself. The last few days they'd been using a makeshift toilet, bathing from a bowl of hot water, and living communally.

Now here he was in the kitchen. Times had indeed changed.

CYRUS WAS HALFWAY across the turning area at the top of the driveway when he heard the back door of the house open.

He darted behind the red Toyota hatchback parked nearby and ducked down. Donald was closer to the house and Cyrus couldn't see him now. He heard a little boy's voice calling out, then Donald's voice.

'Ow, boy.'

JENNY COULD STILL FEEL her blood pressure hovering somewhere near the ceiling, despite Sandy's best efforts, and she knew it would take some doing to get things back to normal.

Not that Sandy was ever going to be her pick of sounding boards in such a situation, but at least she'd given it a good effort. Maybe she wasn't such a bad stick after all.

One thing was for sure – once Mark got home, he'd be getting the bollocking of his life. She didn't care that he was a grown man; you were never too old for a well-deserved bollocking from your mother, and this one was bloody well deserved. There was no way in the world he should have gone after those thugs and left his family behind, unguarded other than by Rob with his pre-historic rifle.

She let her breath out in a hot whoosh, trying to calm down. If she carried on like this she'd have a damn heart attack. She needed fresh air. She stalked to the back door and pulled it open.

ARCHIE HEARD the man call to him and turned, surprised because he didn't recognise the voice.

He saw a rough-looking Maori man in a hoody and track pants standing near the side of the house, only a few steps away from the back door. He had a rifle in his hands and a mean look on his face, and he was looking straight at Archie.

The pig snuffled in her pen, knowing Archie was bringing food to her. He saw the man bring the rifle up towards his shoulder.

The bowl of food scraps dropped from his hand and he let out a scream and ran.

JENNY HEARD two things as she opened the back door. The first was Archie letting out a terrified scream as he sprinted across the lawn towards the other side of the house.

The second sound was the pop of a rifle shot.

'Run, Archie! Run!'

She stepped back inside, moving faster than she had moved for years, all thoughts of her escalating blood pressure and of bollocking Mark gone from her head. She raced towards the hall cupboard by the front door, flinging it open and seizing the shotgun from inside.

CYRUS HEARD a second shot sound and rose up from behind the little Yaris. Donald was working the bolt on the Norinco again, and turned as he did so, a wide grin across his face.

'I nearly got the little fucker,' he shouted. He hurried back towards Cyrus, glancing over his shoulder as the front door of the house opened.

Cyrus saw an old lady appear, a heavyset woman in jeans, sneakers and a mustard-coloured jersey. She had a gun in her hands and was locked onto Donald, who was turning towards her and bringing his own gun around.

'You filthy son of a bitch,' she shrieked. 'You try to kill my grandson? You can just go to hell!'

Jenny wasn't even aware of what she was saying, she just wanted to get this bastard.

She saw his eyes narrow as he turned towards her, then start to pop as he saw she was armed.

She didn't have time to bring the gun up to her shoulder like she knew she should, so she just pointed it towards him and squeezed the trigger.

The shotgun kicked like a mule and she staggered back, her ears ringing from the blast. The guy with the gun staggered backwards, fell on his arse and stared at her in shock.

Jenny jerked the slide back towards her and shoved it forward again, hearing the chunky clack-clack as the action worked a new round into the chamber. She brought the butt up to her shoulder, seeing the guy scrambling away on his hands and knees. Another guy had broken out from behind her car and was trying to help him to his feet.

'You bastards!' she bellowed. 'Have some of this!'

She fired again and saw the standing guy twist and stagger. The first guy got to his feet and staggered after the other one, both of them holding themselves awkwardly as they made a beeline for the paddock.

By the time she had worked the slide a second time the two intruders were in the paddock and limping as fast as they could towards the hedgerow. Jenny brought the shotgun up to her shoulder and took a few steps forward, trying to hold the weapon steady so she could draw a bead on them. It was heavy and her shoulder was throbbing and her arms were trembling but the adrenaline was pumping hard.

She realised that Rob had joined her and also had his gun up in the shoulder. When he fired her left ear went immediately deaf and she fired involuntarily. The wooden fence railings took a hit of buckshot, but the .303 round from the Lee Enfield was more on target, and they both saw one of the guys trip and fall near the hedgerow.

Both of them scrambled beneath the hedgerow and disappeared from sight.

Jenny looked at Rob, realising he was saying something.

'I can't hear you.' She cupped her right ear.

'I said are you okay?' he shouted.

'I think so,' she shouted back, her voice sounding foreign to her.

He scrutinised her face for a long moment. 'You shot them,' he said, his voice quieter now. 'Both of them.'

Jenny nodded. 'Good,' she said. 'The bastards deserved it.' She felt her knees wobble beneath her, and she handed the shotgun to him. 'I think I need to sit down.'

20

The smell of smoke was getting denser in the air, and Shavaunne screwed up her nose. She'd never liked smoke unless she was sucking it up a crack pipe.

They had dropped the car a block back, allowing them to get out on foot and hunt their prey. She was happy enough that they had covered their ground so far, and she was keen to get their patch done before having to regroup with the rest of the family. If her and Dice had to turn up emptyhanded, she'd be seriously pissed. She wanted to come back a winner, lording it over her cousins and proving to Curtis who the real badass was in the family.

They'd slowed down some coming through Takanini, with a riot of sorts going on between a bunch of coons and some soldiers. She'd been in uniform, those blacks woulda copped it. She wouldn't be standing there taking it like the soldiers had, even when they'd busted out some tear gas.

Dice had wanted to get involved but she was driving, so they kept on going. They'd seen Curtis and Lena a while back, but not the boys. Didn't bother her though; they'd catch up soon enough when she was crowing about their success.

Shavaunne looked around her again, seeing the odd person

moving about but nobody coming near her. The sawn-off shotgun in her hands might have been a part of that. She'd never been much on Papakura – too many darkies, for starters – so hopefully they wouldn't be here too long. It was the end of their search area for today though, and being late afternoon, they would need to get back to the car and head for the barn soon enough.

That meant getting their kills soon.

Dice reappeared from behind the building she was standing outside, his face as blank as it always was.

'Sweet?' Shavaunne said, and he nodded his big dumb head. 'Come on.'

They walked up to the next building, a block of five businesses with a service alley behind. Some of the front windows were broken and one, a boutique of some sort, had been looted. Next door was a travel agent.

Shavaunne jerked her head towards the back and Dice followed her into the service alley. Dumpsters and boxes of crap lined the white concrete wall at the back of the building.

They went to the first back door and she tried the handle. Locked. She stepped aside and Dice hit it with a size fourteen boot. The door crashed inwards and she led the way, moving fast through the ground floor. It was empty.

Upstairs was a storeroom and a staff kitchen. Empty again.

They clattered back downstairs and were coming out the back when they both heard it. A stifled sob, behind them. Shavaunne turned, the stumpy shotgun barrels moving with her. She scanned the rear office, her eyes settling on the only other door in the room. It looked like a cupboard and she'd ignored it on the way in.

She crossed to it now, touched the handle and looked to Dice. He nodded, standing ready.

Shavaunne ripped the door open and stepped back, the shotgun coming up. Dice reached in and seized the occupant of the cupboard by her arm, yanking her out and belting her hard across the face at the same time. She was crying already and wailed even more when he hit her, and he threw her against the wall. She was an Asian girl, maybe mid-twenties, with long dark hair. Blood dripped from her newly-split lip onto her white blouse.

'Not her,' Shavaunne said, lowering the gun.

Dice held the girl by her arm, tight enough to make her wince and cry harder, leering at her. Shavaunne knew that leer, and she gave him a warning look.

'Dice,' she said, 'we don't have time. None of that shit.'

He ignored her and reached out, gripping the neckline of the girl's blouse.

'Dice, no.' Shavaunne knew it was a losing battle – once her brother got the idea in his head it would take a bazooka to stop him. He'd never had a normal relationship with a woman before, but he had a high, and twisted, sex drive.

He ripped the front of the girl's blouse in one go, right down to the waist, exposing her white bra and soft abdomen. He turned and looked at Shavaunne. His lips were drawn back from his teeth and his dark eyes were gleaming. He jerked his head towards the door.

'Go,' he growled.

Shavaunne knew there was no point in arguing. She shook her head and moved to the back door.

'Please,' the girl pleaded as Shavaunne went past her. 'Help me.'

Tears were streaming down her face and Shavaunne could see the terror in her eyes. Shavaunne barely gave her a glance. She knew what the girl was feeling; she'd been there herself, more than once. She felt nothing for her. Shit happened.

She stepped out the back door, closed it behind her, and waited.

21

The afternoon had been frustratingly fruitless, and the atmosphere in the cab of the Ford F-150 was tense.

Curtis was seriously fucked off, and the longer this went on the worse it got. Lena was pissed too but while he steamed, she verbalised, and right now she was about one comment from getting a fat lip.

She must've sensed it too, because she finally shut her trap and took to staring out the window. He wheeled the big truck from Porchester Road, a main route heading south, into a side street that led into Randwick Park. It was a suburb occupied by working class families and beneficiaries, and the only reason Curtis Green ever went there was to make a delivery or recover a debt.

He spotted one of his dealers standing on the porch of his house and gave him a toss of the chin as he cruised up. The guy recognised the truck and immediately moved towards the kerb, something urgent in his body language. He was a fat middle-aged Maori dude with a goatee and frizzy hair.

Curtis braked beside him and Stevie came straight to his open window.

'C-Dog.'

'Stevie. All good?'

Stevie wiped his fat nose on his bare arm, leaving a snot trail from his wrist halfway to his elbow.

'Your boys...they down here?'

'Yeah. Looking for a chick and a dude. On foot, they put down my nephew.'

'Dice?' Stevie looked surprised.

'Jaysin.'

'Oh.' Stevie almost looked disappointed.

'You seen them?'

'On their bikes, yeah.' Stevie slid his gaze away and studied his feet.

'No, the fuckin' chick and the dude. Got packs on, she's got long dark hair in a ponytail. Quite fit. He's kinda geeky, got dark hair too.'

'Na.'

Curtis nodded, knowing there was more. He wondered what shit his boys had got themselves into, and hoped Gunner had got them out of it.

'Where're the boys?'

Stevie let out a lungful of air, his cigarette- and weed-tinged breath blowing into the cab.

'Fuck, C-Dog...'

'Spit it out Stevie,' Curtis growled, 'or I'll fuckin' rip it outta your throat.'

'Fuck, bro...' Stevie gestured down the road further. 'The park... that Mobster cunt...'

Curtis stiffened. 'Spider?'

Stevie nodded, still not looking at him. Spider was a senior member of the Mongrel Mob who lived round the corner. Curtis had done business with him before but he was a conniving arsehole and Curtis had no time for him.

'What's he done?' Curtis' tone was low and full of menace.

'I think...I heard your boys might...might be dead.' He shook his head and finally looked Curtis in the eye. 'I'm sorry, C-Dog...'

The Ford's engine roared and Curtis belted it down the road, tyres squealing as he threw it round the corner into Spider's street. The man himself was in the road, short and wide and wearing his gay-as-fuck Mob patch, talking to one of his hood rats who was perched on a dirt bike. Gunner's bike. They were watching another rat pulling a wheelie from the cul-de-sac end towards them on another bike.

Even at the angle, Curtis and Lena both recognised it as Tyson's bike.

Spider and his sidekick turned and saw them, and both of them immediately started to move. The hood rat pulling the wheelie couldn't see them and kept coming.

Curtis let out a guttural roar and gunned the truck hard. He hit Tyson's bike at full noise, throwing both the bike and the rider into the air. The rider flipped backwards, cracked his head on the asphalt and tumbled. The front wheel of the truck bounced over his torso and Curtis threw the truck into a skid.

The rat on Gunner's bike was almost at the alleyway at the end, which Curtis knew led to a park. If the bike got there he'd never catch it. He gave the gas some guts and cranked hard on the wheel, flicking the tail of the truck around.

The hood rat was angling for the footpath but he was too slow. The rear panel of the big truck caught him side-on, hurtling him sideways through the air into the back of a car parked in a driveway. The bike crashed into the garden and Curtis turned his attention back to Spider.

The fat gangster was frozen in the road, his mouth open as he watched the carnage unfold before him. Shit wasn't supposed to happen like this; Spider did the shit round here, no one else. Specially not that white-bread KKK-lovin' motherfucker Curtis fuckin' Green.

He saw the big truck bearing down on him, realised he was about to get run down, and fumbled to pull the stolen Luger from his waistband.

Too late.

Curtis hit the brakes and smashed into the fat gangster, throwing him backwards into the road. Spider somersaulted, landed on a bent leg which snapped like a twig, and tumbled head over heels until he ended up flat on his back.

Curtis bailed out fast, the Beretta tactical shotgun in his hands.

Spider's chest was heaving and his eyes were everywhere. His jaw started moving as soon as Curtis appeared above him.

'I-I-I-I...fuck...C-Dog....'

Curtis snicked off the safety and rested the barrel of the Beretta against Spider's forehead. Spider, so named not for the large web tattooed on his neck but for the fact his surname was Webb, pissed himself.

'What'd you do, Spider?'

Spider's mouth moved, but no words came out.

Curtis pressed down on the shotgun, digging it into Spider's forehead.

'Last chance, motherfucker,' Curtis growled. 'What'd you do...to my boys?'

'I...I...didn't do it...C-Dog, honest bro...some chick an'...an' some guy...'

Curtis physically flinched. *Motherfuckers.*

'I just...I...'

'Robbed them.' Curtis' teeth were bared, lips tight, and he was breathing hard. 'You fuckin' robbed my boys when they were dead. Didn't you Spider...you mother*fucker*.'

He pulled the trigger and the Beretta kicked hard in his big hand. Spider's head was obliterated in a splash of red.

Curtis turned and walked to the closest hood rat, the one he'd knocked off Tyson's bike. The young fella was trying to get up, but one of his arms was broken and he couldn't move far.

The shotgun boomed again and the hood rat took a load of buck in the head and neck.

Lena stood silently, watching as her husband stalked past the body and across towards the second hood rat. This one was unconscious from the impact of hitting the car, and never saw the shot coming.

Curtis turned, did a double take, and went back towards the

mouth of the alleyway. She saw him stop short near the garden adjacent to the alleyway. He dropped the shotgun, his knees buckled, and he sank to the ground with an animalistic cry.

Lena put her hands to her mouth and started to run.

'Oh Jesus, no...'

Behind her she heard voices, rough and aggressive, as others came from Spider's house.

Curtis heard too and he turned, stood, and brought the shotgun up to his shoulder. A stream of vitriol like Lena had never heard unleashed as he stalked towards the new arrivals. He took two steps and fired, and again, and again, then two more steps and fired his last round.

Spider's mates had scattered and Lena could hear screaming, but Curtis was far from finished. He reloaded as he walked, passing her without even a glance, slipping rounds into the tubular magazine from his jacket pocket. Lena turned and saw that one of his targets had been hit and was staggering down the road, clutching his leg and yelping. He wore a Mob patch and black jeans and carried a length of chain in one hand.

Curtis bore down on him like the Grim Reaper, catching up just past Spider's place. He whipped the shotgun across the back of the guy's head and dropped him, then slammed the butt into his head once he was on the ground. He lifted a boot and stomped the guy's head once, twice, three times.

Lena could see from where she was that the guy was out of the game but Curtis didn't stop. More stomps to the head, kicks to the ribs, then one last kick, a full-on toe punt to the side of the guy's head. Lena had nothing good to say about mobsters, but even she cringed at the brutality of the assault.

Her husband left the dead mobster and turned his attention to Spider's house, unleashing shots at it while she went to the side of her dead son. Tyson's eyes were half closed and she could see his neck was twisted at an odd angle. She turned away, raw emotions boiling over, and her gaze fell on a figure in the park, a few metres past the end of the alleyway.

Lena's nose and eyes were streaming and she wiped her sleeve over her face as she half-ran, half-staggered up the alleyway to Gunner's side. He was lying on his side and crusted blood covered his chin and neck. His eyes were wide open and his lips – where they were clear of dried blood – were blue.

The surge of emotion that hit Lena was overwhelming and she collapsed beside her eldest son, cradling his head in her hands and crying uncontrollably. Waves of pain racked her body and she wailed like she had never thought she could. She didn't hear Curtis arrive at her side but felt his strong hands as he lifted her to her feet.

He pulled her into him and held her tight, tears rolling down his own cheeks as she trembled and sobbed against his chest. Barely a minute had passed before Curtis pulled away and stepped back. Lena was still sobbing and unsteady on her feet, struggling to comprehend what the hell had happened.

He wiped his nose on his arm, rubbed his face and scowled at her.

'Sort yourself out, Lena. We got shit to do.'

The hollow in Lena's chest got emptier as she stared at her husband. He snorted and spat on the ground, shook himself like a dog and hefted his shotgun. She wrapped her arms around herself and held on, doing her best to get it together.

22

The sound of chanting and crashing grew louder.

At first Gemma had thought she was hearing things, but now she was certain. She dropped her feet to the floor and hurried after Alex to the front office of the travel agency.

'Oh shit,' he said, 'this doesn't sound good.'

The chanting wasn't clear, if it even was chanting, but the crashing was unmistakable. Windows were being smashed, lots of windows, and it was coming from further up the main street in the town centre.

'It sounds like a riot,' Gemma said, her heart kicking up a notch.

'We better get outta here,' Alex said, turning away from the window.

She grabbed his arm. 'And do what, go out there? With that going on?'

Alex paused, reconsidering. 'True. So what, we stay in here?'

She shrugged. 'At least see what happens.'

Engines sounded and two vehicles raced up from the northern end, pulling up not far from the window they were watching from. One was a police patrol car with a pair of cops, the other was a white Military Police ute with four soldiers.

They stopped in the road and debussed, all carrying assault rifles and wearing body armour. Gemma noticed that the cops fell back behind the soldiers – not a bad move, she thought.

The sound of the rioting mob was getting louder and she saw the first projectiles start hitting the roadway around the troops, bottles smashing and bricks bouncing.

From there it went downhill in a heartbeat, the troops all pulling on gas masks. One of the soldiers stepped out front with what looked like a grenade launcher, and fired a grenade towards the mob, who were still out of sight for Gemma and Alex.

He quickly reloaded and fired again, but still projectiles were sailing through the air towards the troops. Shields quickly came out but it was clear that the troops were not going to win this battle unless they upped their use of force.

'Why don't they just shoot them?' Alex wondered aloud, transfixed by the scene unfolding before them.

'Can't,' Gemma said. 'I doubt they'd be able to.'

Alex looked at her. 'So they can shoot looters, but not people throwing bricks at them?'

There was a flash of flame out in the street as a Molotov cocktail burst in front of the troops. The soldiers and cops scooted back and a second firebomb exploded beside them. One of the cops burrowed in the boot of the patrol car for a fire extinguisher but already a third one was flying through the air.

'Jesus,' Gemma breathed, not quite believing what she was seeing.

She could see the tear gas wafting down on the wind, and with it came a renewed volley of bricks, bottles and whatever other missiles the rioters could get their hands on. One of the cops was knocked down and the windscreen of the army ute was smashed and in a few seconds the first of the rioters came into view from the travel agency window.

They seemed fearless of the small group of troops, who were scrambling back and dragging the injured cop with them. Another Molotov cocktail sailed through the air and exploded on the bonnet of the patrol car. A *whoop* went up from the rioters and they surged forward.

One of the soldiers aimed his assault rifle over their heads and fired two shots, the cracks echoing off the surrounding buildings. It served to break the rioters' forward momentum but still the missiles came in, crashing off the road around the retreating troops, some slamming into the shields that the front two held.

The front of the patrol car was ablaze now and the troops were scrambling back fast, one of the soldiers taking a brick to the chest and falling backwards. As he went down one of the others opened fire on the charging rioters, two shots into the closest guy.

The crowd went berserk, some scattering off to the sides or backing up, a smaller number charging forward.

More shots sounded and Gemma ducked back, pulling Alex with her.

'I think now's the time to make ourselves scarce,' she said. They reached the back office and grabbed their bags, heading for the back door.

'Where're we going?' Alex asked, slinging his bag onto his back.

'Not sure,' she replied, reaching for the door handle. 'But we're not safe here.'

She opened the door and took the first step outside.

Two metres away were the huge man and the scary-looking skinny girl who had attacked them in Alex's home.

The girl locked eyes with Gemma and started to bring round a sawn-off shotgun. The big man grunted and started to move.

Gemma slammed the door and bolted back, shoving Alex ahead of her. 'Move, go!'

A hole was blasted in the door behind them as they scrambled into the main office and up the narrow stairs to the second floor. The back door smashed open and they heard their pursuers crashing through the office.

Alex found a fire exit door and shoved through it, leading the way up another set of stairs and out a door to the roof. Gemma slammed the last door behind them and scanned around them. They had been in the end premises of the building and she could see no way down, leaving them only one option – to run across the roof and hope they found a way down. They were half-way across when the access door they'd used was flung open and their pursuers emerged.

More shots sounded from the roadway and the tang of tear gas drifted on the breeze.

'Run!' Gemma pumped her knees and arms, all thoughts of pain gone as she sprinted across the dirty roof after Alex. He didn't need the encouragement, running like the hounds of hell were on his tail.

They reached the edge and skidded to a halt. Below them was a two-storey drop to a dirty alleyway. There was no fire escape.

They were trapped on the roof with two psychos coming for them.

23

The journey back from Meremere was a quiet one, both of us lost in our thoughts.

I was still processing the events of the day so far, and being dog-tired didn't help. I'd barely slept the night before after the shootout with these clowns, then add on today's shootout and it had been a busy day – and it wasn't over yet.

Most people go their whole lives without ever drawing a weapon on another person. Even most cops do too, unless you work the streets of South Auckland. In eighteen years on the job I'd drawn down on plenty of bad guys, and I'd had weapons pointed at me and even been shot at, but I'd never had to pull the trigger on someone.

In the last three days I'd been involved in three shootings where I'd shot eight men, at least five of whom were dead, I'd drawn down on two young punks, and I'd killed a man with my bare hands. That was all before going to Meremere and confronting that lot, ready to kill them too. That was a situation which could have gone horribly wrong but turned out surprisingly well.

The words of the guy from the previous night and the other guy today ran through my head. *You shot us down like dogs.* That was true; I had. Rabid dogs though, savage dogs, not family pets. Self-defence, not sport. They were missing the point. *They* came to *us*, not vice-versa. Supplies would soon be scarce – hell, they probably were now – and people would fight tooth and claw to protect what they had. I had always done that anyway.

Sure, help out a person in need. I'd helped out Brenton and Linda Rees. I'd help out the Van Dijks, or any other neighbour who was genuinely in need, if I was able to help them. If helping them didn't negatively impact my own family. If they didn't come demanding or stealing.

I'd never been huge on self-analysis. I knew myself and I was okay with what I was.

I straightened up in the seat as Bevan came off the highway at Mercer. He slowed right down to negotiate his way around abandoned cars and I kept my eyes open for any hazards. For hazards, read ambushes.

It wasn't an armed man that made us stop, rather a distressed-looking woman. She stepped out from behind a SUV at the side of the road, waving us down. She was wearing a T-shirt and capri pants and had sunglasses pushed up on her head. She was in her thirties and looked like any other middle-class woman.

'Careful,' I said, readying the Rossi.

He slowed and stopped short of her and I bailed out quickly, scanning around us. I couldn't see or hear anyone else around, but I kept half an eye out as I approached the woman. Bevan was behind me, keeping watch.

The woman's eyes widened when she saw me face on, but she didn't freak out.

'Are you a soldier?' she asked, a desperate plea in her voice. She had a distinct English accent, maybe Yorkshire but I wasn't sure.

'No,' I said, 'just a guy. What's wrong?'

'I need...we need help. My husband's gone and we've been here for twenty-four hours, and we have no food or water.'

I could see the stress in her face. 'Where's your husband gone?'

'He went to get help. I don't know where he is now.'

'When did he go?'

She checked her watch. 'Last night, before dark.'

I figured he was probably dead, but I kept that to myself. She probably knew it anyway.

'Where you goin' too, lady?' It was Bevan, distracted from his guard duties.

'We were supposed to be going to Rotorua, that's where our family are. Well, Alistair's family, anyway.' She turned and pointed behind her. 'We live in Pukekawa, back over there.'

The Waikato River ran past, a hundred metres or so away, winding its way from Taupo out to the Tasman Sea on the west coast at Port Waikato. A bridge spanned the river at Mercer, leading to the farming area of Pukekawa.

'Your husband went back home?' I said.

'Yeah. After we crashed here, the car wouldn't start. He went home to get the other car.' She stuck out her hand. 'I'm Amy, by the way.'

I shook her hand and we introduced ourselves.

She led us to her car, a Mazda people mover that rested at the side of the road with the front wing smashed in. She explained that they'd just come over the bridge and were going to fill up at the gas station, when they were hit by a truck racing through with a load of yahoos in the back. The truck carried on and left them stranded. Alistair had set off home on foot and they'd not heard from him since.

'We'd been at home for two days,' Amy explained. 'The kids were getting scratchy, and we were worried about Alistair's parents, so we decided to head over there.' She looked embarrassed. 'Obviously the power's out, but we thought we might still be able to get gas.'

All in all, their plan had been a poor one, but she seemed to realise that so I kept my trap shut.

Sitting in the back of the car were two kids, a boy and a girl. The boy was about twelve with freckles and red hair and the pale complexion to go with it. He had an Anthony Horowitz paperback in his hand and a bored expression, and had the stocky build of his mother.

The girl looked more scared than bored. A couple of years

younger than her brother, she had long honey blonde hair and was tall and lanky. She was cuddling a teddy bear and her eyes were puffy and red.

'Caleb and Mandy,' Amy said. 'This is Mark.'

I had swung the Rossi around to my back, but their eyes still bugged when they saw me. Mandy looked about ready to burst into tears again. I gave them a smile and tried to look non-threatening, but I could see the whole family were on the edge of falling apart. They had bags and pillows on the seat behind them.

'When did you all last eat or drink?' I asked Amy.

'They last drank this morning and ate last night.'

'And you?'

She looked down. 'Yesterday.'

No wonder she was taking a chance with a stranger. Their car was wrecked, her husband was who-knew-where, they had no defences and no plan. They were easy pickings for predators and my only surprise was that they hadn't been taken already.

I walked back to the ute and fetched a water bottle from Bevan. We'd left in such a hurry that I hadn't brought any supplies, but Bevan being Bevan, he had spare water and a couple of protein bars in the cab.

I handed them to Amy and while she and the kids tucked in, I conferred with Bevan.

'We can't leave them here,' I said. 'They'll be picked off or just die.'

'Wanna tow them home to their place?' He pulled a face. 'I haven't got a lot of gas, man.'

'No.' I shook my head. 'Tow them back to ours.'

'What?' He screwed his face up. 'You're gunna look after them. What're you, a homeless shelter?'

'No, but if we leave them here they'll die.' I set my jaw. 'Gemma's out there somewhere and I just hope to God that someone's helping her out. We can't leave them here, Bevan.'

He still wasn't convinced. 'You already got a houseful; where d'you think they're gunna stay?' Realisation crossed his face. 'They can't stay at mine, there's no room.'

I knew that wasn't true, but I had another plan.

'The Macklins',' I said.

Bevan gave me a look and I could see his cogs turning. 'I dunno...'

'Well they're not there, are they?' I pushed.

'I dunno...'

I was losing my patience, and it felt exposed out there on the side of the highway. Who knew if we were being lined up at that second by some arsehole who wanted what we had?

'Where are they and why're you being so fuckin' shifty about it?' I eyeballed him. 'Spit it out Bevan, I'm tired of being fucked around.'

His shoulders slumped and he licked his lips, before looking me in the eye. 'I dunno where they are, okay? They haven't been home.'

'What else?' I pressed. 'What's going on?'

'Nothing.' He was getting whiny now. 'I just...I haven't got much food, so I...'

'You've been taking theirs,' I realised, and he nodded, staring at the ground.

'Yeah, just a little...I mean, they're not there...'

'Right,' I said. 'I get it. Look, it's no big deal.'

He looked up now, hopeful, and I crushed that hope straight away.

'Just don't steal from the neighbours again, and don't fuckin' lie to me. Ever. Got it?'

He nodded, shame-faced.

'If they want to come, they can stay at the Macklins', at least until we get a better plan together.'

'Fair enough.'

I went back to Amy and made the offer. Two minutes later we were hooking up a tow rope to the front of her car.

24

'Fuck fuck fuck!' Alex stared over the side of the building, then looked back at Gemma. 'We can't get down there!'

She nodded almost to herself, glancing behind them. The pair chasing them hadn't appeared yet but she knew it was only a matter of seconds before they did. She turned and looked across the alleyway at the neighbouring building. It was the same height as the one they were on but several metres away, and she knew that trying to jump it would be suicide.

The other option was to stand and fight. Could they take out their pursuers as they came out the door? The answer came as the door burst open and the girl charged out with the sawn-off shotgun raised.

She fired at the same time as Gemma ducked and moved, grabbing Alex's arm and racing towards the front of the building. She reached the front corner and saw that the rioting crowd below them had surged past their building. Some had stopped to smash up the police and army vehicles, and now both were aflame, thick black smoke billowing. She could feel the heat on her skin.

The building next door had a tin canopy extending over the footpath from the first floor, two stories down.

'Go!' Gemma pushed Alex towards the edge, yanking out the

Glock as she turned. He looked at her with horror and she screamed at him, 'Jump for God's sake!'

She saw the girl loading another round into her sawn-off shotgun, the monster with her still lumbering towards them, and she threw the Glock up.

'Back off,' she shouted, 'get back or I'll shoot. Get back!'

The guy had empty hands and she hesitated to just shoot him. The girl snapped the shotgun closed and started to bring it up. Gemma squeezed the trigger and the bullet whizzed past the huge man's shoulder. He paused with a confused look, glanced down at himself, then looked back at her. His face broke into a goofy grin and a low chuckle erupted from somewhere deep inside him. He started forward again.

Gemma fired a second time, hearing a loud crash from some-where behind her, and the girl fired as well. Gemma felt a tug at her side and went to fire again. There was an empty click and she squeezed the trigger again.

The trigger was slack and nothing happened. She stared at the pistol, having no idea what had happened except that the damn thing wasn't working. She turned, took four strides, planted her right feet on the low edge of the roofline and threw herself out. The Glock went flying and her arms were mind milling, her legs running wildly and she was falling through empty space. The tin canopy had taken a big hit from Alex hitting it and was hanging now at an angle.

She hit it with a tremendous thump and immediately it gave way beneath her, sending her sliding on her front down to the footpath. Hands grabbed her and dragged her out of sight behind the collapsed canopy and she looked up to see Alex above her, dragging her by the arm and her waistband. Another shot sounded and pellets pinged loudly off the canopy.

'You okay?'

She nodded, trying to catch her breath, and he helped her up. He fetched the fallen Glock and handed it to her. She rammed it into her waistband and tenderly touched her ribs, which had come to life again.

More shots sounded right beside her, and she saw Alex had the Marlin carbine up and was ripping off shots at the roofline they had just left. He fired half a dozen shots before lowering the weapon and looking at her.

'I don't think I hit them,' he said apologetically.

'They didn't hit us either,' she said.

'They did.' He poked at her bag. 'There. Jesus you were lucky, there's, like, ten holes in your bag.'

Gemma was about to speak but saw that they had caught the attention of some of the rioters, who were now coming towards them. Someone threw a bottle and it smashed on the footpath beside them.

'We need to go,' Gemma said, but Alex had other ideas.

He raised the carbine towards the small group, bellowing, 'Fuck off or I'll kill you!'

They scattered and she grabbed him, hustling him up the footpath towards the town centre. Now that he'd had a taste of firing in anger she didn't need him going all Bruce Willis on it.

They rounded a corner past the Farmers store and ran like hell. All around them there was damage; smashed windows, broken bottles and signs ripped down, the odd small fire and scorch marks where Molotov cocktails had exploded. A pair of vagrants lounged against the front of a cafe, drinking from bottles of liquor. They paid scant regard to the pair running past them.

Up ahead was a railway overbridge, to the left was a street going back towards where they had started from, and over to the right another block was a Countdown supermarket. Gemma knew the police station wasn't far from there and led the way, cutting across the road and angling through a car park. Her lungs were bursting and her legs felt like rubber but she pushed on, Alex running shoulder to shoulder with her.

The supermarket was a scene of destruction and flames were licking from the broken windows at the front. There was a pitched battle going on in the car park between a small group of cops and a larger group of club-wielding and stone-throwing thugs. They could see a police van on its side with the windscreen smashed in.

'This way.' Gemma skirted the car park and ran to the next corner.

The train station was over to the left and the Papakura Police Station was round to the right. She went right and pulled up short at the front of the cop station. A patrol car was parked on the footpath out the front and the glass of the entrance doors was spread across the ground. A metre-high wall of sandbags protected the entrance and a young female cop with an M4 stood behind them, nervously scanning both ways. She swung the rifle towards them when she saw them approaching.

'Armed Police, stop right there,' she shouted, drawing a bead on Alex, who had the Marlin carbine in his hands. 'Put the gun down and get your hands up.'

Alex did as he was told and Gemma raised her hands too.

'Lady, I see you've got a gun too. Take it out with your left hand and put it on the ground. Either of you do anything stupid and I'll shoot you, understand?'

'Got it.' Gemma followed the instructions and stepped away from the Glock, keeping her hands high.

'Identify yourselves,' the cop snapped, keeping the rifle on them from behind the sandbag barrier. 'What're you doing here and why are you carrying guns?'

'I'm Gemma Dobson.'

The cop narrowed her eyes but said nothing.

'Mark Dobson's wife.' Name-dropping Mark was dicey, given his history, but she figured she had nothing to lose.

'The sarge? Sergeant Dobson?'

'That's him.' Gemma glanced over her shoulder then back at the young cop. 'There's two people chasing us and shooting at us.'

The cop lowered her rifle and gestured for them to pick up their weapons. 'Better get inside.'

She backed through the doors after them, and another cop appeared from the shadows of the foyer, a rifle at the ready. Gemma realised he had been covering them too. His eyes ran over her. He was young too, unshaven and with decorative tats on his muscled arms.

'You're Dobbo's wife?' he said.

'Gemma. This is Alex.' She stuck out her hand but he ignored it.

'I'll take point,' he said to his partner and moved to the front doorway.

The girl rolled her eyes and waved for them to follow her through another broken door into the interior of the station. The station seemed deserted aside from them.

'Don't worry about him,' she said. 'The sarge didn't like him much. I like him though, he's awesome. The sarge, I mean, not him.' She jerked a thumb in her partner's direction then made the universal wanking motion.

'You know there's a big fight going on in the Countdown car park?' Alex said. 'And a riot in town? It looked like your guys and the army guys were getting hammered.'

The cop eyed him defensively. 'You think I wanna be standing guard here? We've been under attack for three days now. I've been here the whole fuckin' time. We've been shot at, firebombed, had a car drive through the front, you name it. It's like a friggin' war zone. I was out on the street all night last night – now it's my turn to guard the station.'

'Sorry, I didn't mean...'

The cop took a breath and let it out. 'Sorry. It's a pretty shitty time.'

'We just need to catch our breath,' Gemma said. 'We've had a pretty shitty time too. We're trying to get home.'

'Make yourselves at home,' the cop said. 'Whatever you can find, help yourselves.'

'Don't suppose there's any chance of a ride?' She knew she was pushing her luck, but it was worth a shot.

The cop snorted. 'Sorry, no.'

'How about fixing this?' Gemma handed over the Glock. 'I don't know what's wrong.'

The cop looked at her sharply. 'This is one of ours. One of the old ones – no light.'

'I know.' Gemma explained how she came to have it, and the cop scowled.

'I should really take it back,' she said.

'Please,' Gemma said. 'We've got people chasing us and I've had to shoot...had to defend us with it.'

The cop raised her plucked eyebrows. 'You've shot people?'

'Yes.' Gemma looked her in the eye.

The cop nodded slowly then turned her attention back to the Glock. She racked the slide and nothing popped out. She thumbed the magazine release and held the mag up, showing it still held rounds.

'There's your problem,' she said, holding up the mag. 'It wasn't jammed, but the mag was loose. Maybe you hit the release by accident.'

'I jumped off a roof and dropped it,' she said.

'You jumped off a roof?'

'Yep.'

'That'd probably do it.'

'That was after it stopped working,' Gemma said.

The cop shrugged. 'They're pretty good guns. Lucky you didn't lose the magazine.'

Gemma slid the magazine back into place and racked the slide. The cop nodded approvingly.

Alex found the kitchen and refilled their water bottles while the cop showed Gemma how to clear a jam from the Glock. She went to a store room and rummaged around until she found what she was looking for, a black kydex holster. She helped Gemma thread it onto the web belt of her cargo pants, positioning it on the right hip. The two spare magazine pouches went on the left hip.

The cop found a box of 9mm ammo and helped Gemma refill her magazines, then handed her the leftover rounds. Alex topped up the half-spent magazine on the Marlin and pocketed the other rounds.

Gemma turned to the young cop again.

'Thanks so much,' she said sincerely. 'I really appreciate it.'

'No problem. The sarge always looked after us, so it's my turn to return the favour.'

Gemma could see the young cop was welling up, and she opened her arms, pulling her into a hug. It was an awkward hug with them both wearing weapons and the cop being clad in bulky body armour, but it felt like the right thing to do. The cop held on, getting herself under control again before pulling away.

'Thanks,' she said quietly, wiping her face and taking a breath. 'When you see Dobbo, please give him my regards.'

'I will. I'm sorry, I don't...'

'Pam.' The cop smiled. 'Pam Williams.'

'Thank you, Pam.' Gemma shouldered her bag again. 'Take care of yourself.'

They headed out the front again, wishing the male cop well on their way past. He scowled and said nothing.

'Nice attitude,' Alex muttered as they walked across the road towards a park.

Gemma said nothing, just focussed on keeping one foot in front of the other. They were over half way home now and nothing was going to stop her from getting there.

25

The Macklin house was set well back from the road with a tennis court adjacent to the large, Colonial-style dwelling.

The 200-acre dairy farm extended behind and south of it, away from our boundary. Bevan had been helping the farm worker who lived further down to milk the cows over the last few days.

I got out and opened the high black wrought iron gates, swinging them back so the vehicles could get up the driveway. Bevan swung around and positioned Amy's bashed-up MPV beside the garage, then unhooked the tow rope and looked to me.

'You know the way in,' I said pointedly. 'I don't. Lead on.'

I was still pissed that he'd been stealing from the Macklins and hadn't told me. I didn't know why it bothered me, because I had no issue with doing what you needed to do to survive. Maybe it just seemed a bit too soon to be in that position of desperation. The Macklins were nice people, and I was sure they wouldn't have minded helping out Bevan, or any of the neighbours for that matter. Maybe it was just the fact that he had been sneaky about it.

Either way, it irritated me and made me not trust him.

He led the way in through the back door, using a key. He caught my look and his cheeks flushed.

'They left it under a pot,' he said defensively. 'Wasn't like it was hard to find.'

The house had that closed-in smell that empty houses get. I went through the ground floor and found nothing disturbed other than the kitchen, where Bevan had obviously eaten and left dirty dishes behind.

Amy and her kids came in and while the kids went to explore, we conferred in the kitchen. I pointed out our houses and told her to make herself at home.

'Are you sure they won't mind?' she said, and I shook my head.

'We don't know where they are,' I said. 'You need somewhere to stay, at least for a few days, and at least here you've got some company and security.'

'Thank you so much.' Her eyes were wet and I could see she was exhausted. 'I don't know what we would've done.'

I shrugged. 'Get yourselves fed and watered, and I'll pop back over soon.'

I left them to it and walked home, happy to have a few moments to myself to clear my head. The pressure of the last few days was intense.

I was met in the driveway by Archie and Jethro, both racing down to meet me. Archie's eyes were wide and I could tell he'd been crying. I dropped to a knee and he crashed into my embrace, wrapping his skinny arms around my neck and clinging on like he did as a baby. Between sobs and gasped half-sentences I pieced together enough to know what had happened, and I carried him back up to the house where I was met by Rob, stern-faced and tight-lipped.

'You okay?' I said.

He nodded and ruffled Archie's hair. 'We had a bit of a rough day didn't we, Archie? But we're okay now, and everyone's safe.' His eyes told a different story but I respected him not wanting to go into it in front of the wee fella.

I put Archie down and told him to go inside, and as soon as he was out of sight, I got the full story from Rob.

'I don't where they ended up,' he said, 'but they ran like hell that way.' He pointed over towards the Macklin house. 'I'm pretty sure we hit both of them, so they may be laying in a ditch somewhere or they may have got away. I don't know.' He shook his head and spat on the ground, then gave me a hard look. 'You shouldn't've run off like that.'

I took that on the chin, even though he'd agreed with me at the time. I got it that he felt vulnerable. What had seemed like the right thing to do at the time had backfired badly. If the bad guy had been a better shot...my gut knotted at the thought and I felt sick.

Rob wasn't finished yet. He took two steps, right up in my face. I could feel his hot breath on my skin and the anger was coming off him in waves. He jabbed a finger at me.

'Don't you ever...*ever*...do that again. You hear me?' His hand was trembling. 'You need to think of your family now, Mark. Stop running round like you're the goddamn sheriff.' He jerked a thumb over his shoulder. 'Your son was scared out of his mind, the poor little bugger. He thought he was going to die, and his Dad wasn't there to protect him.'

My gut knotted some more. I knew he was right.

'If those shitheads come back, we'll deal with them. But your job is to stay here and protect your family.' He paused for breath and I could see a vein throbbing hard in his temple. 'You're no good to us dead. And you left us exposed.' He took a step back and looked away. 'You left us exposed,' he said again, softer now.

I swallowed hard, forcing down the guilt and pride and gut-churning disappointment. I took a breath and let it out slowly.

'I'm sorry,' I said.

Rob nodded once, still not looking at me. I started to go inside but paused, and put my hand on his shoulder.

'You're right,' I said.

I went and found my mother and my mother-in-law, both of whom were sipping glasses of gin and looking pissed off. I tucked my rifle into the hall cupboard and came back to them, sitting on the couch beside my mother.

'I'm sorry that happened,' I said. 'And I'm sorry I left you here.'

Neither of them said anything, just glanced at each other, each one wanting the other one to start.

'Hit me with it,' I said.

My mother went first, giving me both barrels. I let her roll, and once she was done, Sandy had her say. Much more restrained and diplomatic than Jenny had been, but the message was the same. I sat and listened, agreed with some of it and tuned out to the rest. I couldn't argue it; my impulsiveness had very nearly cost us dearly. At the very least it had scared them all out of their wits.

I wondered if that moment was the best time to tell them we had new neighbours. Probably not, but I was already in the doghouse, so I told them anyway. Bizarrely, it proved to be my saving grace. Both women downed their drinks, got up and went to meet the new family. I had no doubt that they'd soon be fussing over them and getting them sorted out.

I found Archie in his room, sitting on his bed with a Tintin book and his teddy bear. I sat on his bed and he put his book down.

'I'm really sorry about today, buddy,' I said. I took his hand and held it. 'I'm sorry those bad guys came here, and I'm glad you didn't get hurt.'

He shuffled over and leaned into me, still holding my hand. 'Lucky Nana and Poppa and Granny were here, Dad. They chased them away.' He looked up at me, a look of awe in his eyes. 'Granny even shot one of them, Dad. She got your shotgun and shot him. And Poppa did too.' He shook his little head. 'I don't know if they killed them, though. I didn't see that.'

The knife in my gut gave another twist. A seven-year-old kid shouldn't have to worry about stuff like that. I put my arms around him and pulled him close.

'Granny and Poppa were very brave. The main thing is you're all okay.' I kissed the top of his head. 'You know what?'

'What?'

'I got growled by all your grandparents.' I smiled and he gave me a squeeze.

'It's okay Dad,' he said. 'You can read me a book if you like.'

He scooted over and I sat beside him, leaning back against the headboard, and together we read. Somehow Tintin and Snowy and Captain Haddock made it all better. Tracking the bad guys could wait.

At least for now.

26

D usk was fast approaching by the time Cyrus and Donald reached Meremere.

After running from that old bitch with the cannon they had cut through paddocks to a road where they broke into a farm-house. Both of them had been shot, Donald getting the worst of it. He had buckshot wounds in his side and his left arm, and had taken another hit on the back of his shoulder when they were nearly at the hedge. That one had gone through his shoulder blade and out the front and was bleeding like fuck.

Cyrus had copped a couple of pellets in his back and arse cheeks.

The farmhouse yielded up a first aid kit and they cleaned them-selves up some, and Cyrus did the best job he could of taping up Donald's shoulder wound. Donald was breathing funny from it and he yelled with pain when Cyrus was doing it, but they found a bottle of whiskey in a cupboard and that helped. By the time Cyrus was finished, Donald was half pissed.

They boosted the Mazda Demio in the garage – the easiest car in the world to boost, which both of them had done dozens of times – and gassed it back home. They took a wrong turn somewhere and ended up down near Te Kauwhata, but eventually dragged their sorry ass into the village and pulled up outside the community centre.

Jake was there, with the other boys who were on the raid, and several others. Bongs and pipes and bottles were being passed around and there was a beat box pumping out some heavy bass.

Cyrus and Donald climbed awkwardly from the stolen Demio and were met by Jake, a meth pipe in one hand and a bottle of vodka in the other. He was wasted and pumped for a rumble.

'Where the fuck you been?' he demanded, wobbling on his feet before them, arms out at his sides as if it made him bigger. 'You fuckin' left my brother for dead.'

'We got shot,' Cyrus said weakly, leaning against the car for support. He was really hurting now and could see Donald was worse. Dude looked pale as fuck.

'Yeah? Well, you dead? I don't think so.' Jake took a hit off the pipe, sucking down meth smoke and holding it in for a few seconds before exhaling through his nostrils like a dragon. He used two fingers in the classic *I'm watching you* gesture. 'I fuckin' see youse with my own eyes...you ain't dead. Henry's dead...not you fullas.'

'Honest Jake,' Cyrus pleaded. 'We went to the house after these guys left...went to finish the job, and we got shot up.'

'Show me,' Jake demanded.

They both lifted their clothing to show him their wounds, and he let out a loud 'Hooooly shit.'

Donald was looking sick and he leaned heavily against the car, not speaking.

'You for real,' Jake hooted, 'you got fuckin' shot alright. Who did it?'

Cyrus slid a glance to Donald, but he was out of the game. No way he was gunna argue.

'Was heaps of them,' he said. 'We got like two or three, but we only had that old rifle, and they come out at us. They had like M-16s and shit, man, they fuckin' blew us away.' He shook his head, sucking his teeth as if recalling a painful memory. 'Dogs, bro, they cut us down like dogs.'

'How many of them?' Jake said, still wobbling on his feet. He took a slug of vodka and let some of it dribble down his chin onto his chest.

'Hard to say...' Cyrus racked his brain. If he said too many, they'd know he was lying. Too few and Jake would wonder why they didn't waste them. 'We got two or three eh, so maybe a couple left? They ambushed us, man, shot us in the back.'

He could still see that old bitch and hear the clack-clack of the shotgun being racked. Couldn't tell Jake they got shot down by some old bitch with a shotgun. Bitch musta been ninety years old.

'D-bo ain't look too good, Jake,' someone said, and Cyrus recognised the voice of Harlem, Donald's cousin. He had also been on the raid, one of the chickenshits that had run off and left them.

He saw that Donald was slumped now, down on one knee and holding onto the car like it was a life raft. His jaw was slack and he looked out of it. Last time Cyrus saw him like that, he'd taken mushrooms so magic he shit himself.

'He's a'ight,' Jake slurred, still trying to focus on Cyrus. He tried to take a hit off the pipe but it was burned out. He dropped the pipe, whacked back some firewater instead, wiped his mouth on his arm and squinted at Cyrus. 'So...Cyrus...you left my brother...to die, eh?'

He waved the bottle at the boy. 'Now your mate and you...all shot up. My bro is *dead*.'

Cyrus could feel all their eyes on him, even Harlem and Te, who had been there. He didn't know where the others were.

'Jake, like I said man...all the shit went down, and we carried on with the raid. Me and him.' He tossed his head at the barely-conscious Donald, who was still slumped against the car. 'We went on, against all them guns, and we tried to finish it. Almost finished it, too.' He caught Harlem's eye but the other boy quickly looked away. 'We didn't leave no one to die, Jake. We carried on, didn't come runnin' back home when shit went down, man.'

Jake nodded, staggered a step, and pointed at Cyrus with the bottle. 'So you the hero, eh? You an' him? Eh?'

Cyrus sucked his teeth again and shook his head sombrely. 'Not sayin' we're heroes, Jake. We ain't got patches on our backs. Henry tol' us to do something and we jus' tried to do it, eh? Shit went down, went real bad, and we hadda do somethin', hadda get revenge against them cunts that shot Henry up.' He saw Jake nodding, and pressed on with that angle. 'We ain't lettin' that shit happen to our bros, eh? Can't let that shit happen.'

He looked into Jake's glazed eyes. 'Bandits don't let that shit happen.'

He heard a scoffing sound from Te, a fat boy with wild, curly hair and fish-lips under a wispy moustache. Luckily for Te, Jake was too wasted to hear it.

Jake focussed back on Cyrus. 'You,' he said. 'You an' him...my bro...' He wobbled, shook his head to try and clear it, squinted again. 'You done it...come...c'me 'ere...'

He put up his free hand and Cyrus clasped it, Jake pulling him into a shoulder-hug and patting him on the back with the vodka bottle. Jake stunk of sweat and booze and crack smoke but Cyrus didn't give a fuck.

This was it. This was real.

He saw Harlem and Te scowling over Jake's shoulder and he glared back. He didn't need them. He could feel the spirit of a Bandit inside him now, feel the rough leather of Jake's patch as he clapped him on the back. Fuck them, fuck those chickenshit bitches.

'Hey Jake,' someone else said. 'Jake. D-bo...I think he's dead, bro.'

27

Heading south from Papakura, they had three options; go straight down Great South Rd, go via the suburban-then-rural roads of Opaheke to the east, or head west and cut left to go south down the motorway.

Neither of them fancied the motorway, and Gemma reckoned that GSR, even though it was shorter in a straight line, was too exposed. It was a main suburban thoroughfare with a pretty rough area not far away, and she didn't believe they should expose themselves so much.

Opaheke it was and she led the way, trotting through the suburban area, past a trashed block of shops and down Opaheke Rd, which soon became rural. She slowed up then, noticing that her ribs didn't hurt so much anymore. In fact, all the running and stress and lack of substantial food was physically changing her. Her clothes felt looser and her body felt tighter.

They walked on the road, keeping an eye out behind them, passing houses and lifestyle blocks without being challenged. Relying on her memory, Gemma took a right and they were soon heading into the village centre of Drury, on Great South Rd near the Drury motorway interchange.

Veering away from the built-up area, Gemma led the way across a sports field and behind an industrial area, walking parallel to GSR. They took cover whenever the odd vehicle passed by but nobody caused them any problems and they were soon at the motorway.

Gemma called a halt by a stand of trees a hundred metres or so from the road, got out a water bottle and took a long drink.

'What d'you think?' she said.

Alex looked past her to the motorway, where they could see multiple abandoned vehicles. A concertinaed pile-up of six cars completely blocked the southbound lanes. They couldn't see anyone around the cars, but Gemma kept a wary eye on them anyway. Now that they were effectively out of the city, home seemed so close. She didn't want to have gone through all that they had done the last three days, for everything to turn to shit right at the end. If they pushed on and walked through the night, she reckoned they could be home in the morning.

She crouched at her bag and rummaged around. Producing a Bounty bar, she waved it at Alex.

'Time for a break,' she said, and eased herself to the ground beside her bag. Her body was stiff and sore and she determined that she better not stay down for too long, or she'd never get up.

'Isn't that only for Kit-Kats?' Alex said. He dug out a chocolate bar of his own, and grinned. 'Haha, just like that. A Kit-Kat.'

They sat and ate chocolate, drank water, and ate more chocolate. Gemma realised they hadn't really eaten since breakfast, which seemed like forever ago. So much had happened. They'd nearly been killed by the psychos back in the travel agency and on the roof, they'd nearly killed themselves jumping off the roof, she'd nearly been beaten to death by the guy from the motorbike, they'd nearly been caught up in a riot. They'd run for their lives practically all day, they'd stolen bikes, and they'd been detained at gunpoint by a cop.

Prior to a state of national emergency being declared, none of that had happened to Gemma. Not one single thing. Now all this, in just one day. And that didn't even include the two days prior.

She shook her head to herself. If it wasn't all so real, so real that you could taste the blood and sweat and smell the gunpowder and fear, it would seem unbelievable. But it *was* real. This was how life was now. The unbelievable was the reality, the bizarre was the norm.

She wondered what her sister Carla was doing, her husband Ryan, the girls, Steffi and Rose. Where were they? Were they safe? Were they at the farm – the girls always called the Dobsons' place *the farm*, even though it was only a few acres – with Mark and Archie and their parents? She and Carla had always clashed, ever since childhood, but she would give anything to see her sister right now. To hug her nieces.

She washed down the second chocolate bar and shoved the empty bottle and wrappers into her bag. No need to litter, even now when the road was dotted with abandoned cars.

'At least our bags will be getting lighter,' Alex said, following suit. 'Have you got much left?'

They did a quick assessment of their supplies, working out they had enough food and water for probably another day. As long as they kept making headway, they'd be okay. Any hold-ups could cause them problems.

Closing his bag up, Alex asked, 'So where do we go from here?'

Gemma had been considering that herself. 'I think the safest way will be cross-country. If we go by road we're bound to run into people, but we can get right down near home by cutting across country, and hopefully we won't run into anyone.'

'Across peoples' farms?'

'Mostly, yeah. Although once we get to Bombay there's public ground round Mount William, I guess it's part of the ranges.' She watched him pondering that. 'I guess there's a risk in cutting across peoples' land, but it's probably less risk than walking by the motorway.'

Alex nodded. 'Yeah, I guess so. We haven't met too many nice people so far, and I could do with a break from them.'

'Same. Let's go.'

They stood, hauling on their bags. Alex picked up the Marlin carbine, looked past Gemma, then grabbed her and pulled her down.

'Get down.'

They flattened themselves and she waited, holding her breath. 'What is it?'

'A car, over there.' His eyes were locked onto something beyond her. 'Stay still.'

She lay there, the bag heavy on her back, the holstered pistol digging into her hip. 'Who is it?'

'A car pulled up, by the crash over there. I can't see the driver but the other person got out. Can't see them very well, but I think it might be them.'

Gemma lay still, waiting, trusting Alex to be her eyes. She strained her ears to listen but heard nothing other than bird noise in the nearby trees and the *whup-whup* of helicopter blades in the distance.

She presumed that it was the bad guys looking for them. Somehow they'd latched onto their trail again. Hopefully the motorway crash would deter them. It would be nice to think that, once she and Alex got past that, they'd have a clear run home. Somehow she doubted that would happen.

'Yep...shit, it's them alright,' Alex breathed. 'He's massive, that guy. He's like a mountain. He's looking around.'

'He hasn't seen us?'

'Don't think so...he's got up on a car...shit.'

Alex ducked his head down and Gemma pressed herself into the grass, not daring to move.

'He's looking all around. It's like he knows we're here.'

'Ssshh. He doesn't know we're here.' Gemma sounded calmer than she felt. 'Just hold tight.'

She could mentally visualise the scene behind her but it was frustrating not having eyes on it for herself. She didn't know how exposed they were nor how well Alex was interpreting what he saw. If the bad guys saw them and came running, how quickly would he react? Hopefully fast enough that they could either get away or defend themselves.

She was pretty sure the gun the girl had used was a sawn-off shotgun, and she knew that it would be pretty inaccurate unless they were close up. Although one lucky shot at distance could be all that was needed. She determined then and there that if these two came for them, she would unleash hell on them. There was no way she wanted them getting their hands on her.

'Wait...he's getting down...he's stopped for a piss.' A few more beats, then, 'He's getting back in the car...yep, they're turning round... and they're going. They're heading back up the motorway in the wrong direction...I can't see them now.'

Gemma let out a breath and eased herself up on her elbows.

'These bastards don't give up, do they?'

28

C urtis Green wheeled the red and silver truck onto the footpath and around the pile of shit on the road.

A sofa, broken pieces of wood, a table and a mattress were piled on top of bags of what looked like household rubbish, obviously placed as some sort of roadblock. For what purpose, he could only guess. He saw a group of hood rats standing in a long driveway, watching him as the truck went by. He slowed, eyeing them through the open driver's window, letting them know he saw them. Whatever they had been planning to do, they dropped their nuts and hung back.

The Papakura Military Camp was back behind them now – he'd taken care to work his way around that, having no wish to tangle with the SAS dudes he knew were based there. Those fuckers were lethal, and even though he'd killed four men so far today, Curtis knew his limits.

Four men. Men who had disrespected his family, robbed them and left them for dead. He would happily kill four more for doing that. He'd kill however many he needed to kill. It had been a while since his last hit, him and Lena having stopped and had a couple of pipes after they'd found their boys. He could feel his nerves jangling and he was getting twitchy.

The boys were in the tray of the truck now, wrapped in a tarpaulin. They'd be buried later.

'Hey.' He stared at Lena until she turned away from the window and looked at him. Her eyes were puffy and red and she had a snotty nose. Jesus Christ, she looked fucking terrible. Where had the Lena gone that he used to know? The hot young thing that could suck a golf ball through a garden hose, who had a sense of adventure?

'What?' There was resentment in her eyes.

'Whaddaya mean, what?'

'*What?*' Her tone was tired, irritated. She always did have a mouth on her.

Curtis slowed again, staring at her. He stopped in the middle of the road.

'Don't you fuckin' talk to me like that, woman,' he growled. 'Watch your fuckin' tone.'

'Or what?' Full defiance now, like she hadn't shown in years. 'You'll get me killed too?'

Curtis' eyes narrowed, getting that mean look he got. He knew what she meant. He knew *exactly* what she meant.

His left fist shot out, a straight jab to the mouth. Her lip split under the impact, blood immediately staining her chin, and her head snapped back. He reached over with his left and grabbed her by the hair, yanking her savagely across the wide bench seat towards him. She tensed up but knew better than to fight back.

Curtis' right hand locked onto her throat like a clamp and her breath cut off.

'Don't you fuckin' talk to me like that, you ugly fuckin' slut,' he hissed in her face. 'I'll fuckin' kill you right now. You want me to kill you right now?'

Lena couldn't breathe let alone respond. She clung onto his forearm with both hands, with not a hope in hell of breaking his grip.

'You fuckin' disgust me,' he growled. He shoved her back across the seat. 'Tidy yourself up.'

She looked at him with weeping eyes, a hand to her throat while she tried to get some air into her lungs. She said nothing, but he knew what she was thinking. He turned towards her, ran his tongue around the inside of his mouth, and spat in her face.

'You're nothing,' he said, wiping the back of his hand across his mouth. He turned away and moved off again.

Lena rested against the door, her breathing slowly coming back under control. Her eyes fell to the shotgun in the footwell.

29

Cooking smells were wafting across our property as I trudged back up the driveway, and my stomach gave me a loud reminder that I'd been neglecting it.

Rob was at the barbecue on the deck, a drink in one hand and tongs in the other, Archie at his side. Archie was obviously feeling much better, chattering away while he "helped" Poppa cook dinner. Jethro bounded from my side up onto the deck and went to the boy for a slobbery cuddle.

'Smells good,' I said, following him up.

'It's about five minutes away,' Rob said. He lifted his glass. 'The ladies are nearly ready inside, grab yourself a drink.'

I found the ladies in the dining room, setting the table. They had a steaming bowl of potatoes and another bowl of beans and carrots, both of which I'd last seen boiling on the BBQ hot plate.

I quickly washed my hands, poured myself a short bourbon and water – weak, seeing as how I still needed to be ready to respond – and joined them in the dining room just as Archie came in carrying a dish of meat. There were chicken pieces, sausages and pork chops, more than we needed for one meal. The generator fuel wasn't going to last forever but while it did, we were going to work our way through the freezer methodically, using the red meat last. The leftovers from tonight would be good for the next day.

I helped Archie sort himself out and sat beside him, Granny across from us and Nana and Poppa at the ends.

'So,' I said, cutting into a chop, 'what're you grateful for today, Archie?'

It was a dinner-time routine that Gemma had established, where each night we would share three things we were grateful for that day. It was a good way of seeing the positives when things hadn't gone so well, and also showing each other gratitude.

'Well,' he said, 'I'm grateful to Poppa for cooking dinner...'

The ladies both smiled, knowing that as far as he was concerned, the meat was the main event, therefore Poppa had done dinner.

'And to Dad for reading Tintin with me...and...' Archie skewered a bean on his fork and studied it before shoving it into his mouth. He cocked his head and thought. 'And to Nana and Grandma for cooking delicious beans.' He grinned at them both. 'You make great beans.'

I felt myself smile and saw my mother doing the same. She began to chortle, then her shoulders were shaking and she stopped eating. Rob and Sandy both caught the bug and soon we were all laughing like fools. It was surreal and absurd but, right at that moment, it was the most natural thing and we all needed and we went with it.

My gut ached and I had tears in my eyes and I couldn't stop laughing.

30

B y the time Shavaunne and Dice reached the barn, Curtis and Lena were already there.

Shavaunne pulled in around the back and they let themselves in the side door. With dusk falling it was murky inside the barn, but a couple of hurricane lanterns threw a pool of golden light around a workbench of sorts. A door had been placed across two sawhorses and Curtis was there, sorting out weapons. The smell of food cooking came from the corner, where Lena was hunched over a gas ring, stirring something in a pot by torchlight.

'Made it,' Curtis said. 'Shut the door.'

'Where're the boys?' Shavaunne said, crossing towards him. 'Maybe they got lucky?'

Curtis stopped what he was doing and looked at her. 'They're dead,' he said flatly.

Shavaunne took a step back, grabbing onto Dice's arm for support. The big retard glanced at her then at his uncle.

'Dead?' he rumbled.

Curtis nodded. 'Both of 'em.'

'What...' Shavaunne had a million thoughts tumbling through her head but couldn't think of what to say. 'What the fuck...'

Curtis nodded grimly. 'We gotta bury them.'

'Where...where are they?'

He turned and pointed towards a tarpaulin against the wall. 'There.'

'They...those two...' Shavaunne ran a hand through her greasy hair. 'Those two do it?'

'Don't know.' He gave a thin smile, so cold Shavaunne felt a chill run down her spine. 'But I found three guys who robbed them.'

Dice grunted. 'They dead?'

Curtis nodded slowly. 'Fuckin' A dead, alright.'

'Oh fuck...' Shavaunne looked at her brother. 'Fuck...the gun. They had a rifle, I thought it was a twenty-two.'

'Gunner's Marlin.' Curtis eyed her and for a moment she thought he was going to erupt. Her fingers closed subconsciously over the sawn-off .410 in her hands. If he saw, he gave no indication, just stared at her, his eyes dark hollows in the light of the lamps.

'Spade?' Dice moved forward, looking around. He spied a spade hanging on a hook and grabbed it.

Curtis handed him a torch and he headed outside to dig two graves.

Shavaunne watched him go then turned to her uncle again. Her nerves were jangling like shit and her and Dice had taken their last hit hours ago. Curtis had gone back to sorting out weapons on the makeshift bench. She joined him, stepping over a length of discarded black polythene marked with dirt, which she presumed the guns had been buried in.

He had laid out several weapons, and he looked at her when she came across the table from him. The cold aggression of moments ago was gone, replaced by a smile. He picked up the weapons in turn and showed them to her.

'Since you're first here, you can pick,' he said. 'These are the best I've got. My gold standard. This is a Norinco .223. Looks like an M16 but it's not.'

Shavaunne saw it had a long, curved magazine and looked cool as fuck.

'This is an SKS, a Russian job. This is a Winchester 12-gauge pump action.' He hefted a larger rifle that looked almost like a machine gun but without the ammo belt hanging off it. 'This is a BAR, a Browning Automatic Rifle. It's a three-oh-eight.' Curtis handled the weapon lovingly. 'This is the shit. World War Two GIs used this to fuck up the Japs.' He put it down to the side and grinned at her. 'You can't choose that, that's mine.' He picked up the last item, a stubby gun with an ugly snout. 'This is an M3 submachine gun.'

Curtis put that down too, and rubbed his jaw. 'Never thought I'd need to pull all o' these out for us.'

He didn't mention how he had come to have the weapons. She didn't need to know he'd robbed a militaria collector, taking all his weapons as payment for the guy's son's drug debts. The Luger had come from there too, along with various items bang-sticks he'd stashed elsewhere.

Shavaunne nodded, her eyes lingering on the submachine gun. 'Things are different now,' she said. She fidgeted with her hands, picking at a sore on her neck that she'd been picking at all day. It was red and the skin around it was flaky and scratched and there was smears of dried blood.

'Fuckin' A different, alright,' Curtis agreed. 'We're gunna get some food, get our shit together and in the morning we'll go and fuck these people up.' He hefted the BAR in his hands and patted the receiver like it was a goddamn dog. 'Nobody fucks with the Greens and walks away from it.'

'Fuck yeah,' Shavaunne agreed. She scratched at her sore some more.

'So what one d'you want?' Curtis pressed.

'Huh?'

He scowled. 'What gun d'you want?'

'Oh, ahh...that one.' She pointed at the M3.

Her eyes flicked over to Lena, still hunched over the cooking pot, to the wall, the ceiling, back to the guns. The barn was large enough to hide a couple of trucks, and with no furniture, she guessed they would be sleeping on the ground tonight. She didn't give a shit right now. Her eyes flicked back to Curtis, who was holding the M3 and looking at her with those sly eyes. The bastard knew what she wanted. Fuck, he knew alright.

'All good, Tricky?' he said softly.

Shavaunne scowled. He knew she didn't like that nickname. It was a hangover from a previous life, turning tricks in a gang-run parlour for sweaty men who helped themselves during the down-time. Fuckin' Curtis. She picked at her sore.

'Need a lil' somethin'?'

She tried to hold out, not wanting to give in easy. He knew she'd be out and she knew he'd be holding. He was always holding. Her will of iron lasted about three seconds before she nodded.

'Okay.' Curtis set down the M3 again. 'Whaddaya got for me?'

'Oh c'mon man.' Shavaunne hated the whiny tone in her voice but she couldn't help it. She needed some shit and she needed it now.

'You know the rules, Tricky. I ain't runnin' a fuckin' charity.' Curtis hitched up his pants and reached into a pocket. He came out with a gram bag. Woulda been seven or eight hundy a few days ago.

Shavaunne locked onto it, all thoughts of guns and dead cousins and cooking smells gone from her head. She needed that shit so bad she could taste it. Curtis was still holding it, out of reach but oh so close. The thought flashed through her head that she could just shoot him, right here and now. Everybody knew he was a cunt, who would care? Her fingers twitched and her eyes flicked back up to his.

He was watching her closely and she knew he knew what she was thinking. He fuckin' knew and he wasn't scared. The miserable son of a bitch.

'You got nothin' for me, have you?' Usually it would be stolen goods or cash, but he knew neither was much use right now.

Shavaunne shook her head, anticipating his next move. Not the first time.

Curtis cocked his head. 'So?' He got that smirk on his face, that smirk he got when he knew she was on the ropes.

Fuck it, you son of a bitch. Shavaunne felt her shoulders drop. 'Okay.' The resignation was heavy in her voice. 'After?'

Curtis almost laughed. 'I ain't stupid, Tricky. Now.'

'C'mon, Curtis...'

'Now.' His voice was harsh. He waggled the bag at her. 'Then you get some o' this.'

'Fuck.' Shavaunne looked past him towards Lena, who still hadn't turned around. 'Okay.'

She turned and headed out the door again, Curtis close behind her.

Lena finally looked up and watched them go. Her eyes burned as she watched her husband close the door behind him. She turned further and looked at the guns on the table.

While his wife plotted her revenge, and his nephew dug graves for his two dead sons, Curtis Green went around the side of the barn and violated his niece for a hit of meth.

31

W ith sore feet and aching bodies, Gemma and Alex had called a halt before dusk. They found a spot near a wooded area where they were out of sight of any houses and the road, set up the A-frame tarpaulin shelter like they had on the first night, and got the ground coverings down to be as comfortable as they could be.

Gemma cleared a patch of dirt and set about making a fire, using twigs and moss that they gathered for tinder and preparing some larger twigs for kindling. In her daypack was a snap-lock bag with cotton wool balls and a lighter, and she quickly got the fire going. She carefully added twigs until they had a small but satisfying fire, and the glow of it brought a warm peacefulness that neither of them had felt in days.

Alex opened a tin of baked beans using Gemma's multi-tool, and set it in the embers at the edge of the fire. It gave her an idea, and she took out the can of Coke she'd been carrying since the day before. She downed it as quickly as she could then used the multi-tool to cut the top off.

After rinsing it out, she punched a hole in each side near the top and threaded a green stick through as a handle. She formed two X's with more green sticks and string and dug them into the ground on either side of the fire, half-filled the can with water and hung it over the fire.

'Bloody clever,' Alex observed, giving his baked beans a stir.

Gemma grinned to herself. It felt like a small victory in a shitty situation. Soon enough the water was boiling and she tipped it over a packet of instant noodles in a small plastic bowl she'd taken from Alex's house. She added the flavour sachet and let them sit to absorb the water, before stirring in a can of tuna.

They sat and ate their meals in silence, the first hot meal they'd had in three days, as the night got darker and the breeze picked up.

'Oh my God,' Gemma said, licking her spoon. 'That was fantastic.'

'Best baked beans I've ever had,' Alex agreed. 'I don't even care that I burnt my fingers.' He foraged in his bag. 'Peanut butter sandwich for dessert?'

'Why not?' Gemma took one from him and tucked in. They had hardly eaten all day and she hadn't realised how hungry she was until they'd stopped. She was also not drinking enough water, so cracked open a bottle and determined to lift her intake the next day. All going well they should hit home the next day, and the thought of it made her heart kick with anticipation. She couldn't wait to see Archie and Mark, her parents, and even Jenny-the-battle-axe would get a hug. What she would give to be in her own home with her family, her own surroundings and her own things.

As the darkness became complete, they reluctantly let the fire burn down and sat, watching the embers. It was a comforting sight, warming both physically and psychologically.

By the time Gemma wrapped herself in her blanket and closed her eyes, she had a clear vision in her head and a renewed determination for the new day.

32

The burial ceremony for Henry, Donald and TK had been a rough and ready affair. As with all funerals in their community it had ended with a lot of drinking and drug smoking, the inevitable fights and blood being shed.

The other boy who had been wounded in the shootout, Skins, had taken a swing at Cyrus, and the two wounded boys had ended up rolling round on the ground throwing wild punches and hurting themselves more than they did each other. Jake had sorted it out by hooking both of them, even though he was barely able to stand after a box of 8% bourbon mixers.

Come dawn, some of the mourners were still going. When Aroha got to the community hall to check on the wounded, she found Jake asleep on the porch with a can still in his fist. Two women – gang sluts that Aroha had never liked, despite them being her cousin's nieces – were sitting in deck chairs, still at it. One was slouched over the side, a dead smoke protruding from the greasy hair over her face, muttering something unintelligible. The other was giggling at her and, between swigs from her can, throwing pebbles at her sister. Aroha could see a wet stain at the front of that one's jeans where she'd either spilled her drink or pissed herself.

Aroha frowned and tut-tutted as she went by, grabbing a torch from inside the door of the hall. With no power on, it was still dark inside. Stepping around sleeping and passed-out locals, she made her way to the makeshift first aid station she had set up. Skins, Cyrus, TK and Tintz were all there on mattresses on the floor. Before she got to them, Aroha could smell death.

The boys were passed out, probably with concussion on top of their hangovers, and Tintz was on his side. Completely still. She shone the torch on his face and saw his eyes open, staring blindly. Blood had dried and crusted around his mouth. Aroha bent down and touched his battered face. Cold and waxy, pale in the light. She sighed to herself, pulled the thin blanket up over his face and straightened up.

She manoeuvred her way back to the front door and out to the porch. Jake was snoring loudly and she knew it would be hours before she got any sense out of him.

She stepped past him, past the two drunken sluts, and headed towards her own house.

Things needed to be done, but now was not the time.

J ake Roimata woke with a headache that had only one possible cure.

He prepared a pipe and settled back against the wall of the community hall, his knees up in front, so he could see the main drag. Not much movement at this time of the morning, being just past dawn. Grey light was spreading over his world and the breeze was cool.

He sparked the pipe with his Bic and took the first drag, sucking the fumes up the glass pipe from the bowl. The first hit was never the best in his view; it was just a taster, the sweetener before the nectar. The second and third were what got the juices going and he worked his way steadily, the point of meth gone within two minutes.

Jake had been smoking this shit, more on than off, for close to twenty years. Started as a kid. Weed by ten, mushrooms and acid as a teen, anything else he could get his hands on to try. Nothing really grabbed him that much until meth exploded in the early 2000's, and that was when he found his mojo.

It was everywhere, taking over from weed as the most readily-available drug on the streets at one time, and he got right into it. Fucked him up and he lost some years, had to get dried out and spent some time in a psych ward, but he got through that and came out the other side cleaner and harder.

Decided the best way forward was to harness the dragon. Moved to Aussie, took to dealing it hard-out, earned his patch with the Bandits and worked his way up in the gang. Still using but not letting it run his life. Dudes did that lost their shit, did dumb shit and got locked up, fucked up or dead.

Earned the Sergeant-at-Arms role through sheer brutality. The enforcer of the gang had to be hard, had to be mean, and that was Jake all over. He dealt out more beatings for rule breaks than he could remember, ran the guns, did the standovers, fronted the other gangs when there was trouble. Had one legend rumble with the Angels, put two of them in hospital even with a broken arm. Fucked up some Bandidos, stabbed a cop and got himself a rep second to none. There was no line in the sand with Jake – when it was on, it was on.

His hard work for the gang paid off, earning him rewards he never would have got if he'd taken a different route. More cash, drugs and whores than he could ever have imagined. Didn't help him much though when he finally went down for stabbing the cop. Got ten years, gave up his office as Sergeant-at-Arms to Little Dog, and did his time. Still dealt drugs inside, bribed screws, organised hits. It was a way of life. Got stabbed himself, four different times – one nearly killed him – but kept on coming back. The fact he seemed indestructible just added to the legend that was Jake Roimata. Didn't need a nickname, he was just Jake. Everyone knew Jake.

Boots crunched on gravel and he looked up. Tintz was there, shades on as usual. It was barely daylight and the cock was wearing shades. Jake sighed inwardly. He'd never understood why Henry was mates with the dude.

'All goods?'

Jake put the pipe down and considered the man for a few moments. 'Na. Not really, eh.'

Tintz nodded, scuffed the ground with his boot and sniffed. 'Gotta smoke, bro?'

Jake squinted at him. 'No, I don't gotta smoke, *bro.*'

Tintz looked at him, like he was ready to say something but changed his mind. He scuffed the ground again.

'An' where the fuck were you?' Jake said.

'Whaddaya mean?'

'Where the fuck were you when your best mate, your bro Henry, was getting shot up? Where the fuck were you?'

Tintz looked offended and set his jaw. His fists bunched. Before he could reply, Jake was at him again.

'Yeah? That it? You get all fuckin' staunch with me eh, but where were you when your bro was getting killed?'

Tintz was puffing now, getting proper mad. Jake didn't let up. It had been bothering him that Tintz hadn't been there, that Henry had died with a bunch of the young boys. Nobody there to watch his black ass.

'You scared, bro? That it? You rather let ol' Henry go out and do the dog work while you stay nice and safe back here?' Jake got to his feet and stepped down to the same level, nice and easy. A few people were traipsing out now, hearing what was going on. Someone watched from a window across the road.

'I ain't fuckin' scared, bro,' Tintz growled., but there was an unmistakable waver to his voice. 'Don't...just fuckin' don't say that.'

'Or what?' Jake spread his arms and looked around him. 'I don't see your army, bro. So what if I speak the truth? People know, they know what you are Tintz.' His eyes narrowed and he stepped forward, game face on now. 'You're a fuckin' coward.'

Tintz huffed and clenched but knew well enough to keep his mouth shut.

'See?' Jake looked around at the people watching. 'This is it; this is the truth. This faggot's a fuckin' coward and he let my brother die.'

'That's not true, Jake,' Tintz snapped, the waver gone now. He was no Jake or Little Dog but, like them, he was a career criminal who'd been in more than his share of scrapes. He was smart enough to be scared of Jake, but he also wasn't going to be slagged off like that, especially not in front of his bros. A rep was earned hard and lost easy, and he could see his circling the drain right now. Fuckin' Jake.

'Oh, eh?' Jake sneered at him, almost laughing.

'Yeah.' Tintz huffed and puffed a bit, considering his next move. There was a lot riding on it. For a moment it seemed like Jake was gunna let it slide and Tintz felt a flicker of relief.

Then Jake smirked and made a wanking motion. Tintz snapped.

'And where the fuck were you, bro?' he demanded. 'You reckon I left Henry out on his own – where were you?' He saw Jake's lips go tight and knew he'd tipped the scales. Fuck it, too late now. 'Why weren't you with him, eh bro?'

Jake took two steps forward and unleashed hell. A flurry of straight jabs to Tintz's face smashed his shades and knocked them off, snapped his head back and sent him stumbling backwards, desperately trying not to go down. You go down and you're dead, and he could tell that Jake was intent on that.

Tintz managed to get his dukes up and block a couple but he was outgunned and in the shit. Jake came forward like a wrecking ball, fury in his eyes and his blood up. Tintz knew he'd made a fatal mistake with that one comment but he couldn't take it back now – he just had to try and hang in there as best he could.

Jake had delivered more beatings in his life than he could remember, and this was going to be the mother of all beatings if Tintz dared to try and fight him. He smashed his fists into his opponent; face, head, gut, ribs, whatever target presented itself to him. Tintz managed to throw a loose fist now and again but he was backpedalling flat out, and even though some of the punches landed they had no power behind them.

Tintz backed into the side of a shit-box Falcon parked at the side of the road and tried to sidestep, but there was no time.

Jake was on him, gut punching him – right, left, right, left – and a monster right hook as he started to slump. The lights went out even before he hit the deck like a sack of shit.

But it wasn't over.

Jake's boots came in, slamming into his ribs, gut, back, legs, then stomping, working up the body to the head. He gave his first boot to the head and was winding up for the second when a hand took his arm.

He whirled, fists up, ready to deal to whoever dared to interfere.

Aroha's rheumy brown eyes stared into his face, and she was frowning. His fist stopped halfway to knocking her head off.

'That's enough, Jake,' she said firmly. She squeezed his arm. 'That's enough.'

'Nan,' he growled, his breathing laboured. 'He...'

The old lady nodded. 'I know what he said, my boy. I know what he said. But that's enough. We got a burial to prepare for, eh? Been enough blood spilled here.'

Jake sucked in air and looked down at Tintz. The gangster was motionless on the ground, bleeding from his nose and mouth and from cuts to his face. Jake didn't know if he was dead, or maybe he would die later. Who knew; who cared?

He gave a short nod and stepped back, releasing Aroha's grip on his arm. Been a time she would've whooped his ass for fighting. No more, but she was still his Nan.

Aroha turned and gestured towards some of the boys watching.

'Here, you boys. Come and pick him up. Get him inside.'

They jumped to it, and Jake watched as they carried Tintz's unconscious form into the hall. Aroha turned to him.

'Go and get yourself washed up, get some breakfast.' She patted his cheek. 'Eh, boy?'

Jake wiped a hand over his face. 'Yeah, Nan.' He took her hand from his cheek and squeezed it. 'Okay.'

34

There days with no sign of Gemma was driving me crazy. I'd expected her to be home by now, and knowing what was happening out there filled me with dread for her wellbeing.

It was possible that she'd gone to a friend's house and was holed up there, or maybe a cop station. Civil Defence would have been mobilised and she could have been caught up with them. Maybe she was still making her way home – by the state of the roads, she was probably on foot – and would arrive at some stage soon. Or maybe she wasn't coming home.

That thought wasn't one I could afford to entertain. To do so would change the playing field, and it was a rough pitch already. Archie was hanging out to see her too, and Rob and Sandy, and even my own mother was concerned. The events of the day before had had a profound affect on us all, one I hadn't anticipated at the time.

My mother had gone quiet and I knew she was working it over in her head, processing it all. I had tried to debrief it with her and give her some perspective, but she was a stubborn old mule and I don't know if she took much onboard from what I said. Maybe I wasn't the best person for the job; I wasn't having much of an issue so far with my own actions. Probably my previous experience helped with that, but I believed it was more of a mindset. I had no problem fighting violence with violence. I wasn't a thug who went looking for it, but when it happened, I could deal with it.

My mother, on the other hand, was in her late sixties and had never entered my world before. Hearing about it and living it were different beasts.

Sandy and Rob were shaken but seemed okay, and I wasn't too concerned about them. The wee man, Archie, had barely left my side. He'd slept in my bed and woke with a bad dream at one point, and I'd cuddled him and got him back to sleep. We'd taken our time in the morning, reading a couple of books in bed and eating breakfast together.

We had walked around the property after that, checked on the animals and fed them, collected some eggs and threw a ball for Jethro. It was as close to a normal weekend day as it could get, if I hadn't been wearing a gun belt and carrying a rifle.

Archie had wanted to see the pistol and I had let him handle it once I'd unloaded. He had grown up around guns and wasn't scared of them, but he did have a healthy respect for them and had fired the Ruger 10/22 before. When he was older he'd be getting his own .22, but with the way things were now, it may be coming sooner rather than later.

As we waited for Jethro to bring the ball back, I wondered if Gemma had come across any trouble. It seemed inevitable that she would, and I was confident that she would make good decisions, so hopefully would either avoid danger or work her way out of it safely.

Like Archie, she had handled firearms before – all the guns I had bar the Browning, which she didn't know about – including a Para Ordnance .45 a mate had brought over for a shoot up. If she found herself in a situation with guns, hopefully she would remember enough to be effective.

Aside from that, I knew she had enough kit in her get-home bag to sustain her for 24 hours. If she had it. She was fit enough and experienced enough at hiking to walk home from the city.

So many variables though, it was impossible to guess. I just needed to be patient.

Jethro bounded back and dropped the slobbery tennis ball at Archie's feet, looking hopeful.

'Gross,' Archie grinned, picking the ball up gingerly. He screwed his nose up at the slobber dripping off it. 'That's disgusting, Jethro.'

'Come on,' I said, 'let's go see what your grandparents are doing, wee man.'

I took the ball from him and we headed back to the house, Jethro nosing at the ball in my hand, wanting more play. I tossed it towards the house and he raced after it. I pulled Archie into my side as we walked and gave him a squeeze.

'Alright there, buddy?'

'Yep.' Archie looked up at me. 'I think Grandma's a bit sad though, Dad. About those robbers that came yesterday.'

'I think you're right, bud.'

'I think I should spend some time with her today, Dad.' So serious and sincere. 'I think maybe she'd like to have some company. After all, I am good at cheering people up.'

I laughed and ruffled his hair, making him smile. 'You are, Archie, you're a good boy. We're very lucky to have you.'

Jethro got the message that there'd be no more ball games for now, so took himself off for a drink instead, while we went inside. The three grandparents were all at the table drinking tea and Archie slotted himself in beside Grandma, giving her one of his cars to play with. She looked at it for a second as if not knowing what to do, and he prompted her.

'That's a Mustang, Grandma. It goes really fast. I got that in a Lucky Dip at the fair, didn't I Dad?'

'That's it.' I watched Grandma give it a nudge with her finger, and she glanced over at me. 'Come on Grandma,' I chided her, 'it goes faster than that.'

She got the hint and joined in playing with him, while I got myself a cup of tea from the flask they had made.

I stood at the bench and Archie and Grandma play together. He was right; he *was* good at cheering people up. One thing that parenthood had taught me was to get over myself, to lose myself in the moment and just enjoy the innocent pleasure of playing with a kid.

They didn't carry the baggage and scars that adults did. They didn't have the same worries and stresses. Financial pressure was deciding which toy to spend your pocket money on, not how long your car could last without a service, or whether you could make the next mortgage payment.

Gemma and I had been through all that, both in our younger years and also after I left the Police. Although I had gone straight into a job, with an overlap between being suspended and actually leaving, it had been a struggle before I really gathered momentum. Another ex-cop had a private investigation firm and took me on contract, doing mostly insurance investigations and security consultancy. It wasn't what I had ever planned on doing but the hours were more regular and family-friendly than policing, and it paid pretty well. As I watched my son and mother play together at the table, Nana and Poppa also watching, my mind drifted back to my departure from the cops.

I'd been a frontline Sergeant at Papakura. It was a night shift. A shitbird by the name of Maurice Panaho, known as Tintz because he always wore sunglasses, had been picked up by one of my crews from a disorder incident. He was drunk and belligerent and gave them a hard time, resisted arrest and they called for back-up.

As with all calls for back-up, the rest of the team broke their necks to get there. I was the first unit to arrive, finding the two young cops scrapping with this clown wearing sunnies out in the street at two in the morning.

They had got a handcuff on one wrist but not the other, somehow he'd broken free from them and he'd managed to get his hands on the OC spray that one of them had drawn.

He'd successfully sprayed one of them and was trying to get the other one when I arrived. One cop was on his knees, nose running and eyes closed, out of the game. The other one had his Taser out and was challenging Tintz. He should've just dropped the prick but he was new and green.

I had approached with my own Taser out. Tintz rode the lightning and it was all over quickly.

Tintz was an associate of the Roimata family from Pukekohe, two of whom I'd had a run-in with on the day the state of national emergency was declared. He had a conviction list as long as your arm, spent most of his life sliding in and out of jail, and was just a general piece of shit.

Half an hour later I was in the Custody Unit at Manukau Hub, waiting for a doctor to arrive and take barbs out of Tintz' flesh. I'd have been happy to rip them out myself but that was against policy.

Seeing me appear in the doorway to the medical room, Tintz had staunched up. The cop guarding him – the same new kid who hadn't Tasered him – had deferred to me and stepped back.

Tintz had recovered from the 50,000-volt ride and decided it was time to share his thoughts on my pedigree. It was water off a duck's back to me, but he made one mistake. He took it too far.

'I know who you are, Dobson,' he said, squared up to me. 'I know where you live.'

'Whatever,' I said. 'Why don't you sit down before you do something you regret?'

'You got a wife,' he continued. 'And a kid. I seen them at the supermarket, doing my shopping.' He flicked his eyebrows at me, his lips curling to expose his rotten and gappy teeth. His sunglasses were off and I could see the boob tats at both eyes. His breath smelled of booze, ciggies and poor health. 'She's a pretty thing. And your boy...' He shook his head and whistled, still smirking. 'I dunno which one of them I wanna rape first.'

And that was that. The line was crossed.

I gave him a good right hook to the jaw and dropped him. The crack as his jaw bone broke was loud and distinct. As he went down he collected a second hook to the side of his face.

The doctor arrived shortly afterwards to more work than originally planned. The young cop, who'd been on my section for all of a week, was easy pickings for the internal investigator and made a full statement, throwing me under the bus. I was immediately stood down and never returned to duty.

Dark days followed, days and nights where I mentally beat myself for my stupidity and lack of foresight. My actions had placed my family in a very perilous position. We faced losing our home if I couldn't get a job. It was publicly humiliating not only for me but for Gemma and the rest of our family. People I had thought were friends distanced themselves, not wanting to be associated with the angry man.

The strain it all put on our marriage was horrendous, and I wouldn't have blamed Gemma if she had pulled the pin. To her absolute credit, she had stuck by me and stayed true. I had vowed then that I would never let her or my family down again. Nothing could ever be allowed to hurt us like it had before.

If we were to make it through this time of martial law, family would always have to come first.

35

C urtis Green woke with a crick in his neck and a sore back from sleeping on the tray of the truck.

He rubbed his eyes and sat up, the dirty blanket falling away to expose his pale, hairy stomach. He scratched his balls and yawned. Lena was sitting in the tray, leaning against the tailgate with her knees up. She was staring at him and her eyes were red-rimmed and baggy. She was chewing on a fingernail, shredding it as she stared at him.

'What?' Curtis sniffed hard, sucked a bogey into his mouth and hoicked it over the side of the truck. 'What's wrong with you this morning?'

Lena said nothing, just stared at him and continued shredding her nail.

'Ah, fuck.' Curtis got to his feet, farted and stretched. The only clothing he wore was a pair of white Jockeys that were fast turning a dirty yellow.

He clambered over the side of the truck and got down, walking unsteadily towards the table where he had last seen food. Sure enough, the gas burner had been at work and there was a pot of boiled water. He found himself a cup, dumped a spoon of instant coffee into it and added three sugars. He poured in the water, stirred it with a dirty knife and looked for the milk. There was no milk.

'Lena, where's the fuckin' milk?'

When no response came, he turned to shout. When he turned round he saw Lena had got down from the truck and was standing a few metres behind him. His shotgun was in her hands and it was aimed at his gut.

Curtis stared at her. 'What the fuck're you doin', woman? Put that down.'

'Son of a bitch,' Lena whispered.

'What?'

'You son of a bitch,' she said. 'You cold...heartless son of a bitch.'

'You watch your fuckin' mouth, Lena,' he warned her, waving a finger at her. 'Now you put that down and stop being fuckin' stupid.'

'I'm not stupid,' she hissed, gripping the shotgun harder. 'I'm not stupid! I know what you're up to, you and that girl.' She gestured past him with the barrel of the shotgun, and he realised that Shavaunne had also got up.

Lena's hands were trembling on the gun.

'I know what you're doing,' she said. Her voice quavered. 'After everything we've been through, all these years...all the shit you made me do...you fuckin' prick.' Tears were welling up and she shook her head. 'You fuckin' prick.'

'Babe, come on.' Curtis tried a different angle, his voice soothing. 'All the shit we did paid for our life...'

'What life?' Lena was incredulous. 'Cars and guns and shit that you wanted to do? Hanging out with cunts who just helped themselves when they wanted a piece?'

Curtis gave a snort. 'A piece of what? Of you?'

The tears were coming properly now, rolling down her cheeks.

'Yes me.' Her voice was small, fragile. 'Remember the parties? All the fucking you thought I wanted? I hated it. I fuckin' *hated* it.'

Curtis licked his lips. He knew very well what she talking about. Years of drugged and drunk parties, girls on the block, everybody having a good time. 'Come on babe, that was just all fun, eh? A bit of drunken fooling around with friends? Nobody got hurt.'

'I got fuckin' hurt,' Lena screamed at him. Her nose running, dribbling snot down her lips onto the stock of the shotgun. The barn was cold and still, the only sound being her sobs. 'I never wanted that. And you got our boys killed. You miserable son of a bitch...'

Her vision blurred with the tears and her shoulders shook as she sobbed. The shotgun barrel wavered and she moved her hand away from the trigger to wipe her eyes.

Curtis moved fast.

In three steps he was on her, grabbing the gun barrel and pushing it away with his left hand. Lena let out a squeal of fright then a grunt as he rammed the dirty knife into her stomach.

Curtis plucked the Beretta from her grasp, withdrew the knife and plunged it in again. Lena stared at him with horror, not comprehending what was happening. Her hands were at her stomach, unable to staunch the blood flow.

'I...I...' she gasped. 'Love..loved you...'

Curtis gave her a look of contempt and stepped back. She grabbed hold of his chest to stop herself from falling but he brushed her bloodied hands away, leaving streaks of red on his chest and gut.

Lena dropped to a knee, breathing hard, her eyes still locked on his. 'I...my...boys...my boys...'

Shavaunne appeared beside her, Dice's big Crane survival knife in her hand. 'You're weak,' she said, her lip curling with distaste. She stepped forward and stabbed her aunty in the ribs, pulled out, and stabbed into her back. Lena collapsed forward onto the dusty floor, groaning and wheezing, and Shavaunne leaned in, stabbing faster and faster, blood flicking off the blade every time she pulled it out.

Within seconds Lena was no longer groaning and wheezing. Shavaunne gripped the knife in both hands and plunged it down one last time, into Lena's neck all the way to the hilt.

She stood again, breathing hard from the exertion. Blood dripped from the blade of the Crane. She licked her lips and wiped a sleeve across her nose. She met Curtis' gaze with a smirk.

'Happy now?' she said.

Curtis scratched his balls and sniffed. 'Helluva way to wake up.' He stepped over to where Lena lay face down on the floor, Shavaunne standing over her. He pulled his undies open and waggled his cock at her.

'You know how to make me happy, sweetheart.' He held her gaze as he began to urinate, the stream of piss splashing down over his dead wife's head. 'And this is what happens to people that cross me.'

Shavaunne said nothing, her eyes shifting down to his member. She wrapped her fingers around the grip of the Crane.

Dice appeared at Curtis' side, that goofy grin on his big dumb face. He looked down at the body of his aunt, then at his sister.

'Shoulda asked,' he grunted. 'Don't use my shit without asking.'

Shavaunne shrugged and handed the knife back to him.

Curtis finished and put himself away. Dice looked at him.

'What we gunna do now?' Dice said.

'Get ridda this.' Curtis looked from one to the other. 'Then we get back to huntin'.'

36

One thing Gemma was looking forward to about getting home was sleeping in her own bed.

As romantic as it sounded about sleeping under the stars, the reality didn't quite meet the fantasy. Not when you were on the ground, top-and-tail with someone you hardly knew, sleeping with a gun in case you were attacked, being hunted by armed psychopaths.

No, she'd be quite happy to put the gun away and slip between some clean sheets with her husband. That said, she had managed a few hours and they were up early, preparing for the day. The shelter was collapsed and packed away, and they straightened themselves up. Her socks felt marginally fresher after shaking them out, beating them against her bag and putting them back on. Just marginally, though. Unfortunately she couldn't do the same with all her clothes, and she was confident she was badly in need of a shower.

Alex must have been having the same thoughts, shaking out his clothes and doing his best to feel a bit fresher.

'A hot bath wouldn't go astray,' he remarked as he pulled his sneakers back on and laced up. 'And a nice breakfast.'

'We've got a nice breakfast,' Gemma said, holding up a Mars bar from her bag. 'What're you complaining about?'

He managed a smile, but she could see he was just tired as she was. 'At least our bags are getting lighter.'

They sat and ate a makeshift breakfast of snacks and water, before Gemma shoved her rubbish into her bag and stood. She dropped into a downward dog pose and began stretching her calves. Alex watched her and chuckled to himself.

'You could do with some stretching,' she told him and he pulled a face. 'I saw you hobbling at the end yesterday.'

'My feet were just a bit tired,' he said, finishing off a chocolate bar.

'You'll slow us up if you're injured,' Gemma insisted, changing legs. 'I want to get home today; if you slow me up I might have to leave you behind.'

Alex grumbled to himself, but he got up and joined her. He groaned again as he started to stretch out his aching legs.

'See? You're not too young to stretch.' Gemma stood and pulled a foot up behind her for a quad stretch.

'Yes, Mum,' he said sarcastically. 'How old d'you think I am, anyway?'

Gemma considered that for a moment. 'Twenty-six.'

He looked up at her awkwardly from his downward dog. 'Wow, really?'

'Too young?'

'No, bang on.' He squinted at her. 'And I'd say you're...'

'Be careful,' she said. She dropped her foot and grabbed the other.

'Thirty-three?'

Gemma gave him a questioning look. 'Really? You're sure about that?'

Alex stood up, shaking out his legs. His face was flushed, but she couldn't tell if it was with embarrassment or from holding the pose.

'Too high?' he asked.

'No, a bit low.' She put her foot down and leaned into a hamstring stretch. 'But it's probably safer to leave it there.'

'Safer?'

She looked at him. 'For you.'

They took a last drink and checked their weapons before shouldering their bags again. Gemma took a last glance around their campsite then looked to Alex.

'We're getting home today,' she told him. 'This was our last night sleeping rough.'

'I hope so,' he agreed.

'We will,' she said firmly. 'We're nearly there, and we're not stopping for anyone.' She hefted her bag. 'Let's go.'

37

The day the Prime Minister declared a state of national emergency after the massive earthquakes and devastation in Wellington, things went to shit very fast.

I'd been given early warning by my brother, Matt, who worked for Parliamentary Services at the Beehive, giving me and my family a head start of about two hours. I hadn't heard from him since, and could only hope that they'd come through it okay. That window of two hours – and I'm sure I wasn't the only one to get the heads up – had allowed me to contact my family and get the ball rolling to make sure we were ready.

In between calling and texting them and picking up Archie early from school, there had been a mad dash around Pukekohe to the supermarket, the hunting store and the gas station.

The results of that mad dash were still not fully unpacked, with boxes and bags of non-perishable groceries still in the garage. The kitchen pantry was full so we set to work getting ourselves sorted out.

It looked like this situation wasn't going to be resolved in a week so we needed to make ourselves as comfortable as possible. Archie passed us items and my mother and I placed them.

The emergency supplies cupboard in the garage already had a

weeks' worth of food, and we filled it to the brim with more. I cleared a shelving unit of tools and painting gear, stacked that to the side, and we filled the shelves with the remaining supplies. Standing back, it looked like a lot. But with five of us to feed, and six when Gemma got home, it gave us a better idea of how long our supplies would last and what we might need.

'A bit more than a month, do you think?' Jenny asked.

I nodded. 'About that, I'd say. Maybe six weeks.' I had never been too good at guessing, but we definitely had more than double our normal fortnightly grocery shop here.

Archie put his hands on his hips and nodded sagely. 'Yep, I'd say about six weeks', Dad.'

I ruffled his hair. 'Good. You in charge of cooking, then?'

'No,' he laughed. 'I'm a kid. I can get my own breakfast, though.'

'And that's helpful, buddy. We all need to do our bit, don't we?'

'Yep.' He nodded again. 'At least 'til Mum gets home.'

I raised my eyebrows and my mother chuckled. 'And then what happens?' I said.

'You know.' He grinned. 'She does it all.'

'What am I, chopped liver?'

He frowned at me. 'I don't know what that means, but Mum does all the household stuff. Anyway, she's better at it than you.'

My mother laughed and I shrugged. 'That's actually true, but it gives me an idea. We need to divvy up some jobs, I think. Come on.'

We took Archie's old blackboard/whiteboard easel into the lounge, he fetched Rob and Sandy, and we sat down to formalise some responsibilities. Being our fourth day without regular power, things were starting get a little out of hand.

Laundry washing was piling up, washing dishes and food prep and cooking were far more laborious than before, and the house wasn't as tidy as it normally was. The thing we'd got really good at in the last few days was using the toilet. A morning ritual had formed whereby we refilled the cistern then we all used the toilet and emptied it with one flush. The males in the house watered the grass outside, while the ladies got to use the throne and let it sit for a single flush later on.

Using the whiteboard, we divvied up duties. My mother took charge of the cooking, Sandy took the laundry and cleaning, Rob took responsibility for feeding the farm animals. Archie took feeding the dog and cat and keeping his room tidy – his normal jobs anyway, but it made him feel included – and I took maintenance and security.

'We've about 5-6 weeks' worth of food,' I said, sitting on the arm of the couch with Archie beside me. 'The water tank is pretty full but I'm going to hook up a couple of barrels to the gutters as well, so we can collect rain water.'

'How much diesel have you got, Mark?' Rob asked.

'As long as we only use the genny sparingly, we'll be okay for a few weeks. Don't want to push it though, and that's high on the list of things we need more of.'

'The neighbours over there,' Rob pointed toward the Macklin place, now occupied by Amy and her kids, 'have they got a tank on their property?'

'I believe so.' Like many larger farms, the Macklins had a fuel tank, but I wasn't sure whether it was diesel or petrol. 'I'll need to talk to one of their workers. We might be able to buy or trade for some.'

'If we don't use the lights and watch TV,' Archie chimed in, 'we can save power, eh Dad? Plus it's also better for the environment.'

'That's right buddy. It means we get to bed earlier because it'll be dark anyway, and we can play board games and read books instead.'

'And we can talk,' my mother said. 'Just like when we were young, before we had TV.'

'In the olden times?' Archie asked, and the older folk all smiled.

'Yep, just like in the olden times,' she said. 'When I was a little girl, we used to go camping with our family. We were in a heavy old canvas tent and we had one lantern that my Dad, your great-grandfather, used to light once it was almost dark. No earlier than that, because it wasted paraffin. We'd sit and play cards or we'd just talk and tell stories, and that was our entertainment.'

Archie's brow was furrowed. 'So no TV then, Grandma?'

'Nope, no TV. Not until I was much older.'

'And no internet either, then?'

'No.'

'Wow.' He looked up at me. 'I know how to play Snap, and Go Fish.'

I grinned. 'Well that's us sorted for tonight then, eh?'

In the interests of hygiene, Sandy loaded the washing machine up. Once the generator was going, she put the machine on a short cold wash.

'Any hand washing's fine,' she said, 'but at least if we can do a load every two or three days we can keep on top of it.'

I went down to the implement shed with Archie and Jethro in tow, and took the opportunity to cut some firewood. We had plenty stacked and dried already, but without knowing how long this situation would last, I went with my usual approach of planning ahead. It felt good to swing the axe and work some muscles that hadn't been worked in a while, and I chopped enough for a week of fires.

Archie used a tomahawk in both hands to try and cut some kindling, not knowing how blunt the blade really was. I kept an eye on him and he worked at it, getting a few sticks of pine cut and tossing them into the wheelbarrow. I cut some more once he'd had enough, and we stacked the logs before taking the wheelbarrow full of kindling down to the house. Being autumn, it would soon be fire season, and we may even need to cook over the fire. I was contemplating the benefits of digging a fire pit when I saw three figures approaching up the driveway.

I recognised Amy and her kids, Caleb and Mandy. I hadn't seen a whole lot of them since Bevan and I had brought them here the previous day. The ladies had been over to welcome them and check on them, and I had seen Bevan there.

We intersected by the house, and I set down the wheelbarrow. Amy gave me a tired smile.

'Been busy?' she said, nodding towards the kindling.

'Yep. How're you guys getting on?'

'Fine, fine. The kids wanted to know if Archie wanted to come and play. Is that okay?'

I looked to him and he nodded eagerly. There was a shortage of kids his age around our area, and he needed more play than I could give him at the moment.

'Would it be okay if they played over here?' Amy asked, and I sensed something more behind the words. 'I mean, they don't really have many toys or anything over there...'

'Sure.' I shrugged. 'Archie, you wanna get your toys out with the kids, or you could play outside?'

He was leading them off before I'd finished speaking, and Amy laughed. It was a short, forced laugh, and I could see the strain and tiredness in her face.

'You okay?' I said. I didn't know her and I had little interest in any personal problems she may have had, but having brought it here also gave me some sense of responsibility.

'Yeah...nah. I guess. I'm just tired.' She ran a hand through her hair and looked away. 'It's...you know.'

I didn't, but I hoped she was going to get to the point. She looked at me.

'You know what it's like. Alistair's gone, who knows where. I don't know whether he's even alive...' Her voice caught and she paused to gather herself. 'He'll never find us here, anyway. Who would come here? And your wife, you know what it's like.' She met my gaze. 'Wondering. Not knowing.'

I nodded. 'I do. You just gotta have faith.'

'Huh. Your wife knows where she's going. Alistair thinks we're still waiting for him back there.'

'If you were still there, you'd either be dead or at least in a bad way by now.'

She shrugged. 'Probably. At least I can feed my kids here, and they have a bed to sleep in.' She rubbed her face then looked at me again. I could see she was chewing something over in her head. 'What if she's dead?' she blurted.

'She's not dead,' I said. 'She's going to make it home soon.'

'But what if...'

'She's not dead,' I said, more forcefully this time. 'It's not a thought I can afford to entertain right now. I believe she'll make it home safely.'

I locked eyes with her and she held it, studying my face. Eventually she nodded.

'Bevan said you were a hard man,' she said.

I shrugged.

'He said not to cross you. He said you'd killed a lot of people.'

I had nothing to say to that, so that's what I said. When she got no response, she nodded again.

'Okay,' she said. 'I'm sorry, I didn't mean to offend you.'

'You didn't,' I said. 'I understand the stress you're under. But don't question my belief, or doubt that Gemma will make it home. She will.'

38

The white Range Rover rolled into Meremere with two outriders on chopped Harleys. Both riders wore Bandits patches and had weapons slung over their backs. The bikes went first, cruising up the main drag to the top before circling and facing back the way they had come.

One stayed where it was, idling, while the other cruised back down, past the community hall where people had come out, attracted by the thunderous engines, back down to where the Range Rover waited.

The bike cruised past it and took up position at the bottom of the road. The Range Rover moved forward, stopping outside the hall.

The rear left passenger door opened and Little Dog stepped out. He was also decked out in his colours, as was Pua, who joined him. Dion stayed behind the wheel with the engine running. Like his four sidekicks, Little Dog had a pistol in a thigh holster, spare mags on his belt. Pua carried a Steyr AUG rifle in his hands and had wraparound shades under the low brim of a cap.

Jake came to meet him and they clasped hands, pulling in for a shoulder-to-shoulder hug.

Stepping back, Jake eyed the rifle in Pua's hands. 'Mean, bro.'

'Eh.' Little Dog tossed his chin towards the hall. 'Where's your bro at?'

Jake sniffed. 'Dead, bro. Got shot up on a raid.'

Little Dog squinted. 'Real? Cops raid you?'

'Na, he and some of his boys went and hadda look at that guy they was talkin' 'bout. Shot him and a coupla the boys.'

Little Dog nodded silently. That gave an extra edge to the reason for his visit. 'Sorry for your loss, my bro.' Little Dog looked skyward, kissed his fist and raised it to the heavens. 'Rest in peace, Henry.'

Jake nodded too, accepting the condolences. 'Good to see you, Dog.'

'We should talk,' Little Dog said.

Jake led the way, the bystanders parting to let the two gangsters through. Pua silently followed close behind. They moved into the kitchen area of the community hall and took seats at a rickety, stained table. Jake lit two smokes and passed one to Little Dog.

'So what happens now, Jake?' Little Dog said, dragging on his ciggie. 'Henry's gone. You callin' the shots round here then?'

Jake exhaled like a dragon. 'That's it. No one else here got any balls to do shit, bro. I gotta look after my town now.' He drew on his smoke again. 'Need to sort that cunt out, the one what hit Henry and them.'

'First job,' Little Dog agreed. He eyed his compadres across the table. 'Gotta be done and done good, eh? Fuck him up, show the rest what happens.'

'Eh, bro,' Jake agreed.

Little Dog exhaled, licked his lips, and showed his yellowed teeth. 'Last time I's here we was talkin' about some guns an' shit. That was Henry's biz though; you interested yourself? That your biz now, Jake?'

Jake blew a grey stream towards the ceiling. 'Gotta be,' he said. 'This cunt's got a fuckin' war arsenal, says the boys anyways. We ain't got shit, they fuckin' lost the ones I had.'

Jake felt it wise just now not to mention he'd actually handed over a weapon. Losing cred with Little Dog would do him no good.

'Uh-huh.' Little Dog stubbed out his smoke on the table, just another scar on the battered surface. 'Well I can help. You see what we got? That's just a taste.' He called over his shoulder. 'Bro, c'me 'ere.'

Pua came to him and handed over his Steyr. It was a bullpup-design assault rifle with an integral scope and a 30-round magazine.

'This is what the army used to use, eh. Looks like a space gun but fuck, ain't no toy. This is the real shit, Jake.'

Jake took it from him and turned it in his hands, admiring it, loving the feel of it. Little Dog saw the gleam in his eye and knew he was on the hook.

'How much?' Jake said.

Little Dog tut-tutted him and handed the rifle back to Pua. He drew the pistol strapped to his thigh and laid it on the table. 'Sig Sauer P226,' he said. 'Army used to use these too. Now they got the Glocks, same as the five-oh's.'

Jake handled the pistol as well, aiming it at the wall and squinting down the barrel. He put it down again and looked Little Dog in the eye.

'We need some,' he said. 'Gotta protect our village, bro. Plus I need to deal with that guy, whoever the fuck he is.'

'Uh-huh.' Little Dog holstered the pistol again. The whole visit had been planned and well-executed. The bikes, the Rangey, the weaponry. The image screamed power, and that was what Henry had wanted. Little Dog could see it was working equally well on Jake.

When the government had returned the Hopuhopu Military Camp at Ngaruawahia back to Maori ownership thirty years ago, a large amount of stores had disappeared. Included was a significant number of weapons and other ordnance.

Little Dog had a contact who was a former quartermaster, discharged from the Army for stealing. Fortunately, the military cops had no idea how much he had stolen over the years. Having moved on from the stores at Hopuhopu after its closure, he spent another twenty years or so with his fingers in the till, building an impressive stockpile of weapons which he hired out or occasionally sold to the right people.

The former quartermaster still lived at Hopuhopu, sitting on top of his arsenal, and it didn't take much to convince him to open the doors to the Bandits.

Little Dog licked his lips again. 'I can get you the Steyrs and the Sigs, no problem. I could get you a delivery of them by tomorrow.'

Jake's eyes gleamed and he listened intently. There had to be a catch coming. He'd done enough weapons deals when he was the Sgt-at-Arms to know that nothing came for free. Being a former office holder in the gang didn't change that.

'How much,' he said.

'Market rate for a Sig? Ten grand. Steyr's twelve.'

Little Dog was pitching high, but not too much higher than he would have done a week ago. There was a shortage of pistols in the country, so they always fetched a premium. Assault rifles were easier to get, even since the law changes, but full-auto military weapons were a different category again.

Jake said nothing, waiting. There was no way he could pay that much and they both knew it.

'You mentioned machine guns before,' he said.

Little Dog nodded. 'Can get a Minimi,' he said. 'Take a few more days, pretty hard to get them, eh?'

'How much?'

Little Dog considered that for a moment, rubbing his chin. 'More'n twenty,' he said. 'Hafta check that one with my guy.'

Silence sat between them for a long minute, neither man wanting to make the first move. Little Dog knew Jake needed the guns, had nowhere else he could get them. Jake knew Little Dog wanted something. Whoever made the first move exposed weakness, showed their eagerness. Eventually Jake figured they couldn't just sit there all fuckin' day. Little Dog already knew he was keen anyway.

'So what's it gunna be?' he said, leaning forward, elbows on the table. 'I ain't got cash for that. You know it same's me. What's it gunna be, Dog?'

Little Dog crooked a grin. They'd known each other too long to play games. Trust Jake to get straight to the point.

'A'ight,' he said. 'Got a issue, affects the club. Got some boys in Spring Hill.'

Jake nodded. He knew that. Spring Hill prison was eight kilometres south of Meremere, next to the Hampton Downs raceway, and was home to a thousand low to high-medium security prisoners. He'd done time there himself and knew it well.

'They still there?' he said.

'Yeah, got them on lockdown. What I hear, some of the screws've gapped it, but some still there. Some inmates broke out when the power went down, but they still got a lot under lock and key, old school.'

Jake eyed him across the table. 'Wanna get 'em out?'

'Aye.' Little Dog sucked on his lower lip. 'Ain't seen any of our boys out yet, but we get 'em out, we in a good position to call some shots. See what I'm sayin'?'

Jake did, and he liked it. But he knew there was more to it, so he waited.

'Get them out, we got guns, we got numbers. We get patches out there, people know we callin' the shots, eh? Cops on the run, Army's out there now. But they ain't give a shit about towns like this...all round here, heaps of places we can loot. Get all the shit we want, set ourselves up. When this all blows over we all good.'

'Looters get shot, bro,' Jake said.

Little Dog gave a snort. 'Huh. Fuckin' Army boys all scared little kids. They see a buncha badass motherfuckers like us turn up, all gunned up and shit, they ain't gunna wanna do shit. They do, we cap 'em, same as anyone.'

Jake absorbed this, nodding. He wasn't convinced on Little Dog's assessment of the soldiers, but that didn't make the plan any less appealing. If there was ever going to be an opportunity to run riot with little to no risk of being caught, it was now. The gang's pad in Papakura would be like the Playboy fuckin' mansion.

'So we do this together, get out the boys, what then?' Jake had his game face on now, knowing this was getting down to the business end.

'That's the thing.' The slightest hint of amusement danced behind Little Dog's eyes. 'You want back in?'

Jake's face gave nothing away, but his mind started racing. He'd figured that could be on the table, but the way it was being sold wasn't right. The Sergeant-at-Arms didn't make offers like that; he dished out the discipline and did the heavy lifting. This was The President's job, maybe the Vice.

'What's Horse say?'

Little Dog showed his yellowed teeth again. 'Nothin'. Horse is dead, bro.'

Jake raised his eyebrows but said nothing. He saw where it was going now, and mentally kicked himself for not seeing it earlier.

'You put him down,' he said flatly.

'Eh, bro. I fuckin' put him down a'ight. I put a cap in his head and that's that, eh?'

Jake tried to slow his brain down. It was a big call to take out the Prez. Caused a lotta shit. 'What about Marty?'

'Marty ain't interested, bro. Handed in his colours straight I did Horse.' Little Dog's eyes were dark and fixed. 'No Prez, no Vice, jus' me. Leo in the big house, got no Treasurer neither.'

Jake nodded, trying to keep up. This was crazy shit, right here. Never had the Bandits had a coup like this before.

'So you're the new President,' he said.

'Aye. Need a team, though. You want in, I'll give you office.' He spread his hands. 'Vice or the muscle, whatever you want.'

Jake nodded again. It was pretty clear where things stood. He also doubted that, if he turned down Little Dog's offer, he'd walk out of this room alive.

'I'll be your Sergeant-at-Arms,' he said.

'On, bro.'

They stood and clasped hands across the table.

39

B y the time Curtis had got himself dressed, splashed some water on his face and had a piss, the youngsters had loaded their aunt's body into the tray of the Ford F-150.

They had her wrapped in a tarpaulin and looked to Curtis as he came back into the barn.

'Wanna bury her?' Shavaunne said, fidgeting with her hair.

'Na, can't be fucked.' Curtis scratched his balls and belched. 'Dump her somewhere later. Don't wanna be connected to her if this all blows over in a few days.'

'Ain't gunna happen,' Dice said. He leaned against the tailgate of the truck.

'That right, genius?' Curtis picked up the pump action Winchester and tossed it to him. Dice caught it in one giant paw. 'I stayed alive so long by not making assumptions. Mostly stayed outta jail, too.' He smirked. 'Mostly, anyways.'

He picked up the M3 submachine gun from the table and tossed it to Shavaunne. 'Don't you fuckers shoot each other by accident, right?'

Dice pumped the slide of the Winchester with a satisfying *clack-clack*. He grinned and rested the barrel over his shoulder. Curtis watched as Shavaunne fiddled with the M3. She looked up at him with a frown.

'How the fuck does this thing even work?' she grumbled.

He walked over to her and took the weapon, showed her how to cock the bolt, flicked off the safety, and settled the skeletal butt against his hip. Standing this close, he could smell her. She needed a wash but, shit, so did he.

'Just point and shoot,' he said, pointing the barrel towards the barn wall. He depressed the trigger and the M3 jumped into life, spraying the tin wall with holes as he hosed the barrel from side to side.

Shavaunne jumped and clapped her hands to her ears. Dice jumped too, but he squeezed the trigger when he did. The Winchester boomed and birdshot blasted several more holes in the roof.

'Fuck me Jesus!' Shavaunne yelled, and Curtis let out a hoot of delight.

'Keep your finger off that trigger, sunshine,' he said to Dice, who was rubbing the side of his head where the barrel had thumped him. Never mind that he'd probably blown his eardrum, the big dumb fuck.

Curtis dumped the empty magazine and handed it to Shavaunne. 'Load that.'

They secured the spare ammo for their own weapons, and Curtis loaded the extra weapons into the back of the truck beside his wife's corpse. He barely gave her body a glance. Far as he was concerned, it had been a long time coming. Maybe now he'd have a better run at Shavaunne. That girl was hooked so bad on the smoke, she'd do anything for a hit.

'Right,' he said, turning to his niece and nephew. 'We know where this bitch lives, right, so she'll be heading there. If they're still on foot they're either there already or still on their way, prob'ly get there today. I don't give a fuck if we get them on the way or once they get home, but we're gunna get them.' He eyed each of them carefully.

'Watch yourselves though, that bitch already killed your brother, killed my boys, tried to kill you too.'

Shavaunne nodded her understanding. Dice looked blank. He could've been sleeping with his eyes open or working on Pythagoras' theory, who knew.

'You see them, you kill them,' Curtis said. 'Unnerstand? No fuckin' around. You go left from here, I go right. You don't find them by night-fall, we meet at Mercer, by the gas station. If none of us got 'em, we go to their house and do it there. Got it?'

'Yep.' Shavaunne fidgeted with her hair some more, jittery like she was, and he could tell she needed some.

Curtis reached into his bum bag and removed a gram bag. He tossed it to her and her eyes lit up. 'Gotta pipe?'

'Yeah.' She looked at her brother. 'Let's go.'

They headed out to the car and Curtis went to get in his truck, hearing a shout from outside as he was about to climb in. He grabbed the BAR and ran for the door.

Shavaunne and Dice stood by her car, staring at it. Dice was chuckling to himself, his massive shoulders shaking, while Shavaunne looked about ready to shit a brick.

The Skyline's passenger side windows were blown out and the panels on that side were peppered with bullet holes.

'You fuck,' Shavaunne shouted, turning on her uncle. 'You shot my fuckin' car to shit!'

Curtis eyed her coldly, the big BAR in his hands. 'Watch your fuckin' mouth, Shavaunne,' he rasped. 'Already killed one lippy bitch this morning – don't make it two.'

Dice stiffened ever so slightly and the air felt heavy. Curtis shifted his gaze from her to him, then back again. 'Load up and get going,' he said. 'I'll see you at Mercer tonight.'

He turned on his heel and went back inside the barn. Shavaunne threw the bird at his back then turned to glare at her brother.

'Dunno what the fuck you're laughin' at, you dumb shit. It's on your side.'

THE SOUND OF AUTOMATIC FIRE, accompanied by a louder boom, sent Gemma and Alex diving to the ground. They were crossing an empty paddock with no cover around aside from long grass.

'What the hell was that?' Alex whispered, hugging the dirt.

'I don't think it was at us,' she whispered back. 'Sounded too far away.'

'Was that a machine gun? Maybe it's the army?'

'That one shot sounded like a shotgun.'

'How d'you know? Oh, of course – your husband has a shotgun.'

'That's right.'

He looked at her, still flat on the ground. 'Does he have a machine gun as well? Maybe that's him, come to rescue you. Or us.'

'No, he doesn't have a machine gun.' Gemma pushed herself up to look around. 'He'd probably like one, though.' She got to her knees. 'I can't see anything; let's carry on.'

They moved off, heading towards a copse of trees at the end of the paddock. A road over to their left was home to sporadic houses, and the motorway was some distance away to the right. Gemma wasn't exactly sure where they were, but the Bombay hills rose up ahead, still a few k's away, and she was heading for them. Get over them and she could easily navigate home. She could almost taste it now.

A minute or so later, the sound of a roaring car engine reached their ears.

40

Spring Hill Correctional Facility was set back off the main highway, a couple of minutes' drive from the offramp. The self-service gas station at the offramp was scorched and the bowsers were knocked over, as if there'd been some kind of explosion. Hampton Downs Raceway was to their right as the convoy headed towards the prison, the whole place looking like a ghost town.

The convoy was led by two hogs, with a Ford Ranger full of thugs behind them. The white Range Rover came next, then another Ranger, an Audi full of heads, and two more hogs. Every man – they were all men – in the convoy was armed, and they had one plan.

They were going to bust open the prison, no matter what.

Jake was beside Little Dog in the back of the Range Rover, a new Sig on his hip and a Steyr between his feet, muzzle up. He had his shades on, the Bandits patch he had treasured for years, and a head full of crack. The crack was good because it made him sharp. He missed nothing and nothing scared him.

He glanced over at Little Dog. 'All goods, Mr Prez?'

Little Dog grinned and nodded. 'All goods, my bro. Gonna get the brothers out, fuck up some screws, and burn that fuckin' place to the ground. That's the truth, my bro.'

'Aye.' Jake nodded and turned back to the window. It felt good to be back in his gears, riding with the boys. This was what it was all about. All the shit he'd had as a kid and growing up, the beatings, the neglect, the sexual stuff – none of that mattered no more. It was all blocked out once he became a Bandit. They wanted him and he needed them. They were his family, always had been. Always stood by him. Forever Bandits, Bandits forever. Henry had never really got it, walked his own path instead. A thug, a badass criminal, yeah, but Henry was no Bandit.

Jake sniffed and his mind flicked back to Tintz. The cunt was dead; good. He deserved it. Jake had no regrets about that.

'Coming up, LD,' Pua said from the front seat.

The vehicle slowed and soon they came to a stop. One of the front riders cruised back to them and Little Dog buzzed his window down.

'Got soldiers up ahead, by the entrance,' the outrider said over the loud rumbling of his engine. 'Checkpoint or something.'

'How many?'

''bout four. Got guns.'

'Any more past them?'

''nother one in the car park by the looks, got a army truck there and I saw two more dudes. They saw us. Might be more inside.'

Little Dog nodded. He turned and looked at Jake. 'On?' he said.

Jake nodded. 'It's on.'

Little Dog turned back to the outrider. 'Jake's comin'.'

Jake got out, the Steyr in his hands, and walked forward. He past the last outrider and saw the checkpoint. A Pinzgauer armoured car blocked half the road, a sandbagged chicane blocked the other, and wooden barriers were ahead of that. Four soldiers were visible, two of them with a light machine gun. The armoured vehicle also had machine guns and shit on it, more than the Bandits could handle.

'Stop there,' one of them shouted as Jake approached.

Jake slung the Steyr over his shoulder and put his hands up to chest height. He was out front of the boys, alone, facing The Man. The Sgt-at-Arms was a man to be feared and shit like this would re-cement Jake's rep in the gang. Showing fear was not an option.

'You the boss?' he shouted back.

'State your business,' the soldier replied.

'Come to give you an option. Come talk to me.'

'State your business,' the soldier repeated, more forcefully.

'Oh, suck my dick,' Jake growled. 'I ain't here for fuckin' Tiddly-Winks, bro. Come talk, get this shit sorted out.'

'Put your weapon on the ground. Any dumb moves and we'll open fire.'

Jake did so, laying down his rifle and pistol. The soldier who had been addressing him came forward now, keeping his rifle trained on Jake's chest. He stopped a few metres away. Jake could see two stripes on his arm – Corporal. He was a tall white boy in his early-twenties. He was in full battle kit with a ballistic vest, helmet and webbing. He was weathered and looked like he knew what he was doing. The name on his chest read Schinkel. Great – a Nazi motherfucker. Nothin' a black man liked more.

'What're you here for?' he said.

'We come to get our bros outta jail,' Jake said simply.

The soldier shook his head. 'That ain't happening,' he said. 'The prison's on lockdown and we're in charge.'

'Martial law eh?'

'That's right.' The soldier tossed his chin towards the convoy behind Jake. 'Who you got here?'

Jake glanced casually over his shoulder. 'These're my boys.'

The soldier ran an eye over him. 'Turn around.'

Jake did so, coming back to face him.

'Bandits, eh?' The soldier's lip curled. 'You supposed to be a gang?'

Jake bristled. The cheeky fuck. 'You ain't hearda the Bandits, you gotta problem,' he growled.

The soldier laughed. 'Whatever, mate. Your buddies aren't getting out, so turn yourselves around and go back to where you came from.' His eyes hardened. 'We see you here again, we won't stop to talk. Understand?'

Jake eyeballed him. 'You're makin' a mistake. We don't give a fuck about anyone else, we just want our bros out. You needa make that happen.'

The soldier laughed again. 'I don't think so, mate. Don't try and intimidate me with your bullshit. We're the fuckin' Army, mate. We kill people for a living.'

Jake gave a slow nod. 'Your call,' he said.

He turned and walked back, scooping up his weapons as he did so. He got to the Range Rover and went to Little Dog's window. It buzzed down and Little Dog eyed him, his face like stone.

'Yeah?'

'Not today,' Jake said.

Little Dog's face went tight. '' the fuck?'

Jake shook his head. 'They know what they're doin'. They got bulletproof vests and all the shit. We go against them right now, they'll mow us down. We need a better plan.'

Little Dog scowled. This wasn't how it was supposed to go. The Bandits didn't back down to no one. He took a breath and considered what Jake had said. Jake was no fool. The Sgt-at-Arms was the enforcer, but he was also the leader in battle. If he said it wasn't on, Little Dog had to trust that.

'A'ight,' he said. 'But we'll be back.'

'For sure, bro,' Jake said, a hard glint in his eyes. He had never liked backing down. 'We'll be back, and we'll take these mother-fuckers.'

Jake moved down the convoy to spread the word, and the vehicles slowly turned around. As they moved back towards the highway, Corporal Schinkel watched them go, a thoughtful look on his face. He turned to his crew.

'Heads up, boys,' he said. 'They'll be back. We see them, we shoot them. Got it?'

There were nods and murmurs all round. Schinkel hefted his MARS-L rifle. This wasn't exactly Afghanistan, but he had a feeling it was heading that way.

41

The Van Dijk's over the road were always happy to receive visitors, and when I went over, I found Clyde and Ellette there. The conversation broke off as soon as I appeared in the doorway, and all eyes turned to me. Rusty gave a small smile and Sophie looked to their visitors.

'Morning everyone,' I said, 'sorry if I'm interrupting anything.'

Ellette stood, closing her cardigan over herself and looking at me stiffly. 'We were just leaving anyway,' she said.

Clyde got to his feet as well and ran a disapproving eye over me. Disapproving was the only way Clyde knew how to look at me.

'Is there really any need to carry that thing around?' he said, looking at the rifle over my shoulder as if it was a snake poised to strike.

'Yep,' I said. 'I think so.'

He pursed his lips. 'You know what, Mark?' he said. 'This is a difficult time for us all, but people like you just make it harder.'

I raised my eyebrows. 'How's that?'

'All this violence and shooting and everything.' He looked like he was about to cry, and Ellette wrapped her cardigan tighter around herself. Maybe it was a ballistic cardigan. 'Normal people aren't used to it and we don't like it. This is not our life.'

'Yeah, I know that. It's not how it should be,' I agreed.

His mouth was open, ready to deliver the next pearl of wisdom, but he stopped when I agreed with him. 'What?'

'I said it's not how it should be,' I said. 'If people behaved properly and didn't go round stealing and robbing and shooting people, we'd all be much better off, wouldn't we?'

'I...I...yes, of course...'

'But since that's not the case,' I continued, 'people like you need people like me to keep the bad people away.'

He pursed his lips again, pissed that I'd played him. It was an age-old argument and one that neither side would ever concede. Bleeding-heart liberals like Clyde only saw people like me one way.

'That's not what I meant, and you know it,' he snapped.

'I know what you meant,' I assured him. 'You want someone to cover your arse and stop the badness, but you don't wanna see it or hear it or smell it or taste it, right? You wanna be able to live in your ivory tower of righteousness and point out all that's wrong with the world, and talk about how terrible it is and look at those poor misunderstood people who never had a chance, the ones who were maligned by society, and harassed by the police, the ones we all sponsor through the taxes we pay from the jobs we do every day, the ones born with their hands out who just keep on taking and taking...'

'Don't...' he started, and I cut him off with a glare.

'I'm not finished yet,' I said. 'Those poor disenfranchised people who's only option in life is to take from the workers? They have choices to make, same as everyone else. They can choose to be a taker and a waster and sit on their arse whinging about how unfair life is, or they can get up and get a fuckin' job and actually contribute to society.'

'I...'

'And if they come and try and steal from me or hurt my family, then they face the consequences of that decision. Same as you. I don't care who it is. And people like you, Clyde? You sleep well at night because people like me are out there. You don't want to hear about it, but you sure as hell want to sit in judgement of us when it suits. But you know what, Clyde? Fuck you.'

He recoiled, and a condescending look came into his eyes.

'Don't come to me for help. You have any trouble, you just sit down and have a good talk with the bad people, maybe form a committee or a review team. Don't ask me to help.' I tore myself away from him and turned to the Van Dijk's, who had been listening silently. 'Sorry guys, that's not what I came over here for. I'll come back another time.'

I turned and stalked out, surprised at how angry I'd got so quickly. Guys like Clyde gave me the shits, and that would never change. I saw Bevan heading towards the Macklin house but I ignored him and kept on walking. I wasn't in the mood to talk to him right now. I had intended to do the rounds of the closest neighbours, just a quick welfare check to see how they were all doing, but my run-in with Clyde and Ellette had changed that.

I made my way home instead and found Linda and Brenton on the drive, talking to Sandy and my mother.

'Just the man we came to see,' Brenton said as I joined them.

'That so.' If they wanted something, they were going to be shit out of luck. I'd lost interest in helping others today.

'Have you got any spare water tanks?' Brenton asked, and I immediately frowned. He wasn't off to a good start.

'Why's that?'

Linda frowned at my terse response, then realised what I was meaning.

'Oh, no, nothing like that,' she said with a laugh. 'We're not asking you for anything. It's just, we have some.'

'And what, you want a hand hooking them up?'

'No, no,' she said. 'We were going to offer them to you.'

'Oh.' I hadn't seen that one coming.

'Take a breath, my son,' Jenny said, with that condescending tone I hated. The second person to speak to me like that in the last few minutes. 'You're only trying to help, aren't you, you two?'

'Yeah.' Brenton studied me. 'Sorry if we offended you mate, but we have a couple of spare barrels and we wanted to offer them to you, since...you know.' He shrugged. 'You've helped us out.'

My cheeks got hot and I felt like a fool. I tried to force down my embarrassment. 'Ah...thanks. I do have a couple that I was going to connect up to the spouting, so if you need them...'

'We've got four,' Linda said. 'I had this great idea of connecting them all up and using grey water for the garden, but we never got round to it. We're going to hook up two, but there's only the two of us and you've got a houseful here, so we thought you might need the other two more than us.'

'That'd be great,' I said, my mood lifting. 'I'd really appreciate it. I've got the connections and taps for mine.'

'It's settled then. Come down when you're ready, we've got all the piping and stuff.' Brenton gave me a smile. 'You're welcome to them.'

They headed home and I gathered Rob and Archie to give me a hand. I could tell that my mother had something else to say but my mood hadn't lifted far enough to entertain that, so she wisely backed off.

We collected the barrels from down the road and carried them home. They were standard blue plastic barrels that held 220 litres each, and had taps already attached at the bottom. Brenton also gave me the spare spouting he had bought and Archie carried that home in a shopping bag.

We placed them around the house and the sleepout, one at each downpipe so as to maximise our catch.

Rob straightened up and wiped sweat from his brow. 'That's very kind of them,' he said. 'And here I was, thinking he was a dork.'

Archie giggled. 'Poppa, you shouldn't call people a dork.'

'That's right, I shouldn't,' he agreed. 'People also shouldn't be dorks.'

Archie went off searching for food and entertainment, and Rob and I set to work. The sun was doing its best to dodge the clouds sliding past and there was a light breeze, but even so it soon became hot work. I rested my rifle nearby and stripped down to my T-shirt.

It didn't take much to divert the downpipe into the first barrel, going through the hole we cut in the top. Once the barrel was full with run-off from the guttering, any excess would flow through the second pipe we inserted and connected back to the downpipe. The barrel stood on stacked bricks to allow better access to the tap.

Doing the manual work took my mind off the run-in with Clyde and Ellette, the pressures of the situation we found ourselves in, and the fact that Gemma was still out there. Somewhere.

Rob finished sealing off the two inserts with silicone to prevent leakages, and I stepped back and surveyed our work.

'Not bad,' I said. He gave a satisfied nod.

With the average person needing three litres of water a day for cooking, cleaning and drinking, this barrel alone, once full, gave seventy-three days' worth of water for one person. The four barrels together would supply our family – once Gemma got home – with enough water for forty-eight days. With winter coming around the corner, there'd be no issue with them being filled.

Normally set-ups like these were used like how Linda had planned, simply for irrigation, but water was water and it was essential for us to secure as much as possible. We couldn't just order a delivery by truck anymore when we ran short.

Rob poked my arm with the silicone tube.

'Come on boy,' he said. 'Got three more to do.'

Sandy poked her head out the door and hailed us for morning tea. I smiled to myself. Even with things the way they were, she always got morning tea ready at ten a.m. I could bet it was cheese and crackers and a cup of tea. The routine was familiar and comforting.

42

Gemma and Alex made their way through the copse of trees to find themselves at the edge of a rural road.

The road was empty but they could see a couple of houses further down on the left and another up on the right, where the road crested a hill and dropped from sight. Across the road were more fields rising up a hill, cattle grazing peacefully.

'It's very quiet here,' Alex said.

'Welcome to the country, Alex,' Gemma said with a smile. 'This is what it's like.'

'I have *been* to the country before,' he said indignantly. 'I know what it's like.'

'Okay.' She shrugged. 'You don't need me to tell you to watch out for that wasp nest then?'

He looked around doubtfully then jumped back when he saw the large nest of paper wasps on the trunk of a pine beside him. 'Jesus, that's huge.'

'I know you saw it, but...'

He grumbled under his breath as she led the way across the road and over the wire fence into the paddock. Gemma waited patiently while Alex clambered awkwardly over the fence. He paused at the top, staring gingerly at a single strand of wire that ran parallel to the fence.

'Is that electric?'

'It was, it's not on though.'

'How d'you know?'

Gemma resisted the urge to roll her eyes. 'I touched it with a piece of grass. Besides, the grid's down, isn't it? Unless they've got solar power, it wouldn't be on anyway.'

'Or a generator,' he said, still wobbling in place on the fence. 'They might have a generator.'

'I just told you it's not on,' she said. 'Hurry up.'

Alex got both feet onto the top wire and tried to jump, but he slipped and landed with a thud on the ground. He groaned, tried to get up and put his hand in a cow pat. He cursed and looked up at her, only to find his companion laughing at him.

'It's not funny,' he complained, wiping the crap off on the grass. 'It's alright for you.'

Gemma put out a hand to help him up, pulling it back when he stuck out the hand he'd just wiped. 'Other one.'

She helped him up and he dusted himself off and picked up the Marlin he'd dropped.

'Are you alright now, poppet?' she said.

Alex frowned. 'Don't call me poppet just because I'm gay,' he said.

'I'm calling you poppet because you're behaving like a child,' she retorted, softening the jibe with a smile. 'Come on, nothing's broken.'

'Only my pride.' He grinned reluctantly and rubbed his shoulder.

'Let's get going before you break a nail.'

The cows watched them go by with nothing more than a passing interest, and they soon reached the top of the hill. Ahead of them lay a block of farmland with another road a few hundred metres away. A stream cut through the paddocks near the road, and more cattle grazed. Farmland extended out on all sides. Further ahead were the Bombay hills.

Home was not far on the other side of that, and Gemma felt a surge of energy. They were nearly there.

She turned to Alex. 'We're so close now.'

He was about to reply when they both heard the crack of a bullet pass between them, close enough that they both felt the wind. The report followed a split second later.

They dropped as one, a second bullet passing overhead.

'Who the hell is that?' Alex cried.

'No idea.' Gemma tried to look while she stayed flat, but couldn't see a thing with the long grass around them. 'We need to get out of here though.'

She started to crawl forward, the way they had come, using her elbows and toes to move. Alex followed suit, a third shot sounding.

'It's coming from our left,' Alex said. 'Maybe those houses?'

'More likely someone on foot,' Gemma said, doing her best impression of a commando.

They reached the start of the downward slope and kept going, gathering some speed. A fourth shot sounded and the bullet thudded into the dirt off to their left.

'Trespassers!' a man shouted from that direction. 'Get off my land!'

He followed it with another shot, this one hitting the ground to their right.

'Run,' Gemma said, pushing herself up, 'go!'

She threw herself into a dead run for the fence to their right, a standard wire and batten number that divided the paddocks. She could hear Alex behind her as she pumped her arms and legs, going for gold. She didn't hear the next shot but felt the wind past her head.

She planted her hands on the top rung and swung her legs over in the most graceless hurdle she'd ever done. She tumbled to the ground and rolled awkwardly, the day pack pushing and jerking at her back as she moved. Alex hit the ground in a heap, swearing to himself, and Gemma already had the Glock out in both hands, arms extended, searching for their hunter.

Maybe the second paddock wasn't his and he'd just give up.

Another crack told her that wasn't the case. She could see him now, on the far side of the paddock they'd just left, a rifle at his shoulder. He was wearing a blue and black patterned fleece like hunters wore, and was on the other side of the fence, maybe fifty yards away now. With a hunting rifle, he could pick them off easily.

She wondered if they could call a truce and just back away if he only wanted them off his land. She was about to shout to him when he fired again and one of the battens in front of them splintered.

A splinter of wood ripped across her cheek and she yelped with pain.

'Wanker.' Gemma saw him working the bolt on his rifle. She sighted as best she could at the distance and fired one shot. The guy looked up in surprise and stood stock still. She fired again and he dropped down. 'Go.'

Bent over, Alex ran parallel to the fence line, dropping down twenty metres or so away.

'Cover me,' Gemma shouted, thinking she sounded like a hero in one of the movies Mark liked to watch. She fired again as she got up then she focussed on running, hearing another shot from the guy and a return pair from Alex. She went past him and dropped down ten yards further on. 'Alex, go.'

She scanned for the guy but couldn't see him, as Alex ran past. Mark had told her about "pepper-potting" at some stage and explained why it was done, and she figured it was probably a good idea to do it now, given they were so exposed.

The guy popped up again with his rifle and she fired, making him drop back down. Alex called her forward and she ran again, and they continued on like that until they reached the far end and could no longer see the guy. Pausing to catch her breath, Gemma realised they hadn't been shot at for a minute or so.

'Think he's gone?' she panted, wiping sweat from her brow. She could feel blood trickling down her cheek and wiped that too. The cut stung from the sweat running into it.

'No, there he is,' Alex said, pointing.

The guy was tracking them down his side of the other fence, keeping the distance of the paddock between them. Gemma could see the blue of his top against the green and brown of the paddock.

She glanced over her shoulder and saw that the paddock they were now in was maybe forty metres wide, with a slight slope away from them.

'We can get to the next fence,' she said. 'Back behind us. Get into the next paddock over and it'll be harder for him to see us.'

'You go first,' he said. 'I'll cover you.'

Gemma raced off parallel to the fence line, hearing Alex open fire behind her. She stopped half way and turned, covering Alex as he sprinted towards her. They made it to the next paddock without being fired on and made their way down, heading south again.

They lost sight of the guy and he seemed to have given up. Crossing another fence, they kept on running but Gemma started to relax a little. She could see the road up ahead, just two more paddocks to go, with the stream creating a natural barrier. The cattle grazing in the paddocks seemed undisturbed by the shooting.

'Nearly there,' she said.

43

'The fuck was that?' Dice muttered, sticking his head out the window. 'Someone shooting at us?'

Shavaunne slowed to a crawl, straining to hear. The Skyline's muffler was deliberately loud but she heard another shot – a hefty boom – then a bunch of lighter pops. 'Definitely shooting,' she said. 'Don't think it's at us though.'

'Maybe someone's huntin',' Dice guessed, and she gave him a scathing look.

'And what, the rabbits are shooting back?'

Dice frowned. 'Doesn't hafta be rabbits,' he said.

'For fuck's sake, it doesn't matter. Animals don't shoot back, dumbass. That's a fuckin' shootout.'

More shots sounded and she threw the Skyline around then accelerated back the way they'd come. There were a few houses down that way; maybe shit was going down back there. She gassed it down the country road.

She wasn't sure exactly where they were but the adrenaline was pumping now, mixing with the meth in her system to give her a buzz better even than sex. Definitely better than sex with Uncle Curtis, at least. That fat fucker grunted like a pig and pawed her like she was a piece of meat.

As much as she had enjoyed driving the blade into Lena – her first kill with a knife and, *goddamn*, that was satisfying – she would happily do the same to Curtis. If she could get her hands on his stash, she'd have no further need for him. Plus he'd shot up her car, the fat fuck.

Her and Dice could go it alone, roaming the countryside like Bonnie and Clyde, taking what they wanted from whoever crossed their path. They had guns, wheels and a bad motherfuckin' attitude. It was on like Donkey Kong.

Of course, she'd have to try and manage Dice's raping. He did like it and he had the attention span of a pencil.

They passed some empty fields and got to the first house. A quad bike was parked beside an open gate and nobody was around. They continued on, past another house, and reached a T-intersection. To the left was the way they'd come, heading back towards the barn a k or so away. Shavaunne went right, stopping at the top of the hill. She got out, scanning the countryside around them.

Fuckin' fields and cows and trees and shit everywhere. She fuckin' hated the countryside – it smelled like shit and there were too many bugs that wanted to eat you.

She heard more shots in the distance, beyond the houses they'd just passed. She switched off the engine and listened again, hearing only the ticking of the engine as it cooled. She shaded her eyes against the mid-morning sun and looked, knowing they were out there somewhere. Her gut told her it was the people they were chasing. Who knew who they were shooting at, and who cared? If those two fuckers were there, she'd find them.

'What're ya...'

'Sssshh.' She ignored her brother and continued scanning, working her way across the fields she could see. A minute later a broad smile broke across her face. 'Gotcha.'

She could see two figures running beside a fence, heading south.

It had to be them. She started to turn back towards the car when a flash of blue caught her eye and she wheeled back.

Someone else was there, tracking the two runners. That person, whoever they were, was ahead of them and heading in the same direction. Instinct told her that the person in blue was hunting the two runners, and she felt a kick of adrenaline. No fuckin' way was she gunna let someone else take them down.

Shavaunne turned back to the car and her brother. 'Let's go,' she said.

44

The community hall at Meremere had been cleared of anyone who wasn't invited, and the doors were closed.

A guard stood at the door and everyone else gathered in the hall itself, sharing smokes and drinks. The kitchen door was closed too and Little Dog sat at the table with Jake, Pua and Dion.

Jake knew that the last two were more than just Little Dog's bodyguards; they were trusted lieutenants. The thought had occurred to him that they needed to be watched, but he also needed to build a relationship with them. He'd known them off and on over the years, never been too close though.

He fired up two smokes and passed one to Little Dog. He offered the pack to the others. Both declined. By the looks of their 'roid muscles, these boys would rather hit the bench than the baccy.

'So,' Little Dog said, 'our boys are still in the *hinaki*.'

Jake nodded. A *hinaki* was an eel trap, but was also an old-school term for prison, which was pretty much the same thing. 'We gotta crack this a different way,' he said. 'Them soldiers ain't gunna roll over just 'cause we show up.'

Little Dog bristled. 'Then they ain't met the Bandits before, bro.'

Jake nodded again. No point shooting down the Prez in front of his boys; he had to make this Little Dog's idea.

'What I'm thinkin' is, we be a bit more sneaky.' He rubbed the bristles on his jaw and looked thoughtful. He had the plan worked out already, but Little Dog needed to "help" him with it. 'I'm thinkin' we send a diversion in, maybe a car with women in it. Distract 'em while we come in on a few different angles, lay it on heavy, and go in hard.' He leaned forward, elbows on his knees, and looked up at Little Dog. 'Gunna need some heavy artillery though.'

It was Little Dog's turn to nod and look thoughtful. 'Uh-huh.' He licked his lips then raised a finger to his nose. He inserted it into a wide nostril, dug around, and extracted what he was looking for. He wiped it on his jeans then blocked one nostril at a time and snorted the other, emptying the contents onto the floor. He wiped his nose on his forearm and looked back at Jake. 'Whaddaya thinkin'?'

Jake sat back. Time to get down to business. 'Machine guns. Grenades. More Steyrs. Shitloads of ammo.'

'Gotta outgun them,' Little Dog said, getting into it. 'You gotta make sure when we hit 'em, we do it right first time, eh?'

'Yep, for sure,' Jake said. 'Go all out you reckon, LD?'

'Fuck yeah. We ain't fuckin' around here, bro. They gotta know the Bandits come to play.'

Jake grinned. 'For sure, for sure.'

Little Dog nodded again, but Jake wasn't finished yet.

'Rockets'd be good,' he said. 'Explosives.'

Little Dog's eyebrows shot up his forehead. 'The fuck you gunna do with them?' He gave his sidekicks an incredulous look, laughed, then turned back to Jake.

Jake held his gaze. 'Blow shit up,' he said. 'It's a prison. It ain't like breakin' into a house. We gotta take out the fuckin' soldiers outside, we gotta take out the fuckin' soldiers inside, then we gotta bust out the boys. Might be locked in with steel doors'n shit.'

Little Dog stared at him for a moment, and Jake could practically hear the cogs turning in his head. Maybe he'd pushed it too far. Maybe Little Dog wouldn't go for it.

'Plus,' Little Dog finally said. 'We gotta cap all them screws in there. Can't let them cunts get away. Plus any other fuckers we might find.'

Jake nodded and grinned. It was a fair point. All the gangs were mixed inside; this would be a great opportunity to take some payback. Looked like Little Dog actually was on board.

'When're you thinkin'?' Little Dog said.

'Soon as we get the gear to do it,' Jake said.

Little Dog turned to Dion. 'You know where to go,' he said. 'Take some boys and get what we need.'

Dion stood and left without a word. Jake and Little Dog grinned at each other across the table.

'Just like old times, Jakey,' Little Dog grinned.

'Never had this much fun in the old times,' Jake said.

45

The hum of a bee caught Curtis' attention while he watered the weeds at the side of the road. Not wanting that near him while his pecker was out, he cocked an ear and zeroed in.

Over to the side, floating gracefully between wild flowers, busy doing its thing. Not the least interested in the big man with the shotgun over his shoulder, doing his own thing. Curtis shook, zipped up, and turned away. He opened the door of the Ford then stopped.

Listened again. Listening to people had never been one of his greatest skills, but he was damn good at listening for unusual sounds. Unusual sounds usually meant either the cops were creeping up on him, or someone was trying to rip him off or attack him.

He stood stock still for a few moments, sure he'd heard gunfire. Not close, more over to his left and further south. The eastern side of the motorway, towards Bombay. Shavaunne and Dice should be over there, and if they were, that meant they'd found their prey.

'Fuck yeah,' Curtis murmured to himself, hearing another decent shot. He climbed into the truck and fired it up again, placing the Beretta shotgun on the seat beside him. The BAR was leaning in the footwell. He was ready to rock'n'roll.

He shifted the big truck into gear and hit the gas.

THE ROAD WAS COMING up and Gemma started looking for a way across the creek.

It ran parallel to the road, gnarly old trees lining the low banks, and there was a gap of a few metres the other side before the road. It continued down to the right as far as she could see, going around a bend in the road. To the left it seemed to narrow a bit so she moved that way.

'Shall we jump it or go through it?' Alex asked, looking at the gap tentatively. It was a couple of metres or so wide and was moving pretty well. 'How deep is it?'

Gemma shrugged. 'Don't know, but I don't want to wait around for that guy to catch up. Let's just jump one at a time. If we get wet, we get wet.'

'I can't swim,' Alex said, and Gemma shrugged off her pack.

'Don't worry, I'll go first. If it's too dangerous we'll find another way. But we can't muck around.'

She handed him her bag, checked for the best place, and took a running jump. She landed on all fours on the opposite bank and scrambled to her feet. Alex threw her bag across the gap then his, followed by the Marlin. Gemma waited while he got himself ready to jump, crossing her fingers that he wouldn't end up in the drink. So far, his experience of the country wasn't going great.

'You can do it,' she said, 'you'll be fine.'

He sprinted, leaped and hurtled across the gap with a terrified expression on his face and his arms and legs flying. He landed with all the grace of a drunk, but he was safe and dry.

He was grinning when he got to his feet, but the grin immediately fell and he muttered, 'Oh shit.'

'Don't move, you arseholes,' a man shouted.

He stepped out from behind a tree ten metres away, his rifle trained on them. His blue and black hunting top told them who he was.

'Put that gun down,' he told Gemma, and she did as she was told. 'Get your hands up.'

They raised their hands. 'We were just cutting through,' she said. 'We're trying to get home.' The rifle looked fearsomely lethal so close up, and the man behind it was angry.

'I don't care,' he said. 'It's my property. The last few days, I've had pricks stealing my shit, trying to take my cattle, all that. Bad luck for you that you got caught. You're lucky I didn't bloody shoot you back up there.'

'We're not looking for trouble,' Gemma said, her voice quavering. 'We're just trying to get home. My son is waiting for me. They don't know if we're even alive.'

She felt a sudden rush of emotion and her vision blurred. Her cheeks were hot and her heart was racing. They were so close to being home and now this; it was unfairly cruel. The guy sounded like he was just going to shoot them and be done with it.

The guy paused, considering what she'd said. 'You tried to kill me,' he said, as if he was just realising.

Gemma almost screamed at him. 'Because you shot at us! What'd you think we'd do, stand there and let you kill us?'

He jabbed the rifle towards her, slowly advancing a metre or so. 'Hey, stop yelling at me. You're trespassing on my property and I'm the one with the gun, remember?'

Gemma had had enough. She wasn't going to stand here all day and argue with this idiot. She was tired and sore and scared and just wanted to get home. 'Then just shoot us, you miserable bastard,' she shouted. She took a few steps towards him, waving her arms. Tears were running down her cheeks and she was struggling to form words. 'I've had enough of people trying to kill me...you wanna do it, then fuckin' hurry up and do it.'

She stopped and dropped her arms, crying properly now. The guy stared at her, confused. Alex stayed where he was, hands still in the air, uncertain what to do. Gemma dropped to her knees, her shoulders shaking as she cried. 'I've had enough,' she sobbed. 'I just want to go home.'

The guy lowered his rifle. 'Go,' he said, waving them away. 'Just go. But don't come back.'

Gemma looked up at him through her tears, a background noise registering somewhere in her brain. 'Thank you,' she whispered.

The noise got louder and they all turned to look behind the farmer. A lowered black car was flying down the road towards them.

'Oh shit,' Alex said, 'it's them.'

Gemma scrambled back towards him, getting her footing and snatching up her bag at the same time. Alex picked up his bag and the Marlin carbine, but was rooted to the spot.

The farmer stood transfixed, not sure what was going on.

'Run,' Gemma screamed at them both, 'run!'

SHAVAUNNE SAW THEM UP AHEAD, the two they were chasing and some other guy with a gun. He looked like a hunter.

Beside her, Dice readied the Winchester shotgun in his big paws. 'It's on,' he grinned, 'like Donkey Kong.'

Shavaunne boosted it, closing he gap rapidly, but the hunter guy was raising his gun. The other two were moving. A shot sounded and a bullet cracked the windscreen in front of her.

'Cunt,' she muttered.

Dice leaned out his window with the shotgun and it boomed, but the guy didn't move. Just stood there at the side of the road, fiddling with his gun. The gap was closing. Another shot sounded and the windscreen shattered, glass fragments slicing across their exposed skin.

Both of them yelped and cursed and Shavaunne rammed her foot to the floor.

46

G emma and Alex got across the road into the scrub there, going for the cover of a small copse of trees, as the guy opened fire on the speeding car.

'Jesus Christ,' Gemma breathed, turning as the car bore down.

The farmer was still standing at the side of the road, working the bolt on his rifle, when the Skyline reached him. There was a sickening thump, the last-second screech of tyres, then the farmer was thrown into the air. He went straight up, flipping over as he flew backwards. The car went off the road and became airborne, crossing the creek and smashing into the ground so hard it bounced, landed on two wheels, and flipped sideways onto its roof.

The farmer hit the ground at the roadside with an ugly crunch, his legs still up in the air and his head and shoulders taking the impact.

'Jesus,' Gemma said again, her gut dropping through the floor. Nobody could have survived either of those impacts.

Alex moved forward first, reaching the farmer then reeling back with his hand to his mouth.

'Ohmygod, ohmygod, ohmygod...' He took two steps then threw up, unable to stop himself. Gemma arrived beside him and stopped, feeling her own stomach clench at the sight. The guy's head was smashed like a dropped watermelon and was leaking brain matter and blood. The left side of his face was smashed in and that eyeball was popped out, hanging by pink flesh.

Gemma lost her words and just stepped back, avoiding Alex's puke, repulsed by what she had seen. Across the creek the car engine was still roaring and the wheels were spinning. She could only imagine what horrors that car contained.

In the distance she heard another car now, a big engine, coming their way at speed.

'We need to go,' she said to Alex. 'Come on.'

'What about him?' He gestured weakly towards the body of the farmer. 'We need to help him.'

'We can't help him, he's dead.' She shook him by the arm and pushed him towards the other side of the road. 'We need to go now.'

PRETTY SURE THEY were both concussed, Curtis left Shavaunne and Dice lying where he'd dragged them and went back to the overturned Skyline. Not that a concussion would make much difference to Dice, he figured.

He crouched down and leaned in to turn off the ignition. They were damn lucky to escaped from this wreck with nothing more than cuts and bruises – from what he could see, anyway. The roof was crushed down and it had taken some effort to get Dice out of the passenger seat. Shavaunne had been thrown clear, probably through the windscreen by the look of the cuts on her, and he'd found her lying a few metres away from the car. At least she wouldn't be so pissed about the bullet holes now.

He rummaged through the wreck until he found their weapons and ammo, lugged that over to where they were stirring, and gave them each a nudge with his boot.

'Wake up, dickheads,' he said.

Shavaunne screwed up her face and looked at him, struggling to focus. 'What?'

'Was it those two?' Curtis demanded. 'Or just that joker?' He jerked a thumb across the creek towards the corpse at the side of the road.

'Huh?'

It took several minutes before they had enough of their senses to start talking, and even then Curtis wasn't convinced they were all there. He got enough out of them to come up with a plan.

'Get in the truck,' he said. 'We're going to that address they left. They're not there, we'll waste whoever is, then work our way back towards them. Either way, I'm tired of these fuckers. It's time to end this.'

47

T he cut on Gemma's cheek had stopped bleeding and begun throbbing instead.

They didn't have time for first aid just now though, not with bodies behind them and other psychos somewhere close to their tail.

They had run like hell, crashing through undergrowth without care, copping more scratches and bumps until they reached another paddock and sprinted across it. Fence after fence, through a hedge, across a trickling stream, ignoring the farm track that ran through the property and sticking the safety of the paddocks instead.

Finally, a farmhouse hove into view.

They finally stopped, dropping to the ground in a sweaty mess behind the second-to-last wire batten fence to check their surroundings. Gemma struggled to get her breath back as she scanned around, while Alex glugged back water.

'Don't see anyone,' she panted. 'Can't hear anything.'

Alex wiped his mouth and put his bottle away. 'Have a drink before you pass out,' he said.

She didn't argue, and quickly drained a bottle. 'I'm almost out,' she said.

'Same.'

They scanned again, listening intently, and both shrugged. The house was surrounded by a well-maintained garden and neat lawns.

'Old people,' Gemma said, and Alex nodded.

'Do you want to try there?' he asked. 'Maybe see if we could borrow a car or something?'

She nodded. 'It's worth a shot. Hopefully there won't be an angry farmer like the other guy.' An image of his shattered head flashed through her mind and she closed her eyes, urging it away. She had the feeling that one was going to be hard to shake. 'I'll go first,' she said. 'You cover me from here, and if there's any trouble you better save my arse. We're too close now to screw it up.'

She climbed the fence to the dirt track and took that down towards the house, still not seeing or hearing anything. The house was all closed up and she sensed it was empty. No cat or dog came to check out the visitor.

She went to the back door, staying within view of Alex, and knocked. No reply, and the door was locked. A quick circuit of the house showed that all the windows and doors were secure. She checked through the garage windows and saw a white Honda parked inside. The garage was also locked.

Gemma returned to the back door again and waved for Alex to come forward. While she waited, she checked under the pot plants and rocks closest to the door. By the time he reached her she had found the spare key.

'We can't go in,' Alex said, looking horrified. 'This is someone's home.'

'Seriously? After all the shit of the last few days?' She unlocked the door and pushed it open. 'Hello? Anyone here?'

The air smelled musty and stale and of death. Gemma was reminded of when she and Mark had been around to her grandmother's and found her dead, passed away peacefully in bed. She covered her mouth and nose and went in, Alex hanging back by the door, still not happy about going into someone's home.

She found the sole occupant of the house sitting in her armchair in the lounge, a little old lady wearing a dressing gown and slippers. Her skin was waxen and her white hair limp where it fell across her wrinkled forehead.

Gemma turned away and went back to the door. 'She's dead,' she said. 'Looks like she passed away a few days ago.'

Alex closed his eyes for a moment as if passing a silent prayer. 'Poor thing. I guess there's nothing we can do for her.'

'Nope. We'll lock up and put the key back, but I do want to use her car.'

'We can't do that,' he protested.

The argument that ensued took less than a minute and ended with Gemma threatening to leave him behind.

'We can be at my place in ten minutes by car,' she said finally. 'Or we carry on walking and risk whoever's chasing us finding us. Stay if you want, but I'm going.' She showed him the set of keys she'd found in the kitchen.

'Fine,' he relented. 'It just seems wrong.'

'We'll bring the car back later,' Gemma told him. 'But the sooner we're home, the sooner we're safe.'

48

Little Dog passed the joint to Jake, held the smoke in his lungs as long as he could, and watched his old compadre with half-closed eyes. They were sitting in deck chairs outside the community hall. Pua stood over to the side, alert as ever.

Aroha had been by earlier and wanted to know what they were up to with all the patches and bikes and what-not. Jake had felt bad when Little Dog sent her on her way, but he was the President and that's how it was. She needed to learn her place – she couldn't play the Nan card with the Bandits.

Jake took a hit and sucked it down.

'Sent two of the boys up town,' Little Dog said. 'Gunna get the rest of the boys an' come down. When Dion gets back with the guns an' shit we be good to go, my bro.'

Jake blew smoke and nodded. He passed the joint back to Little Dog. It was just straight weed, nothing too heavy. Just a chill-out after some heavy decision-making. "Up town" meant Papakura, where the pad was. He had no idea how many of the boys would be around to bring back. As if reading his mind, Little Dog gave a lazy grin.

'They gunna swing through Puke too,' he said. 'Pick up your bros and nephews an' that, bring 'em all back down here too.'

Jake felt himself grin. It would be good to have his blood around him.

'Be all set,' he said. 'Get the boys, get the guns, go back and bust that shit up. Be a thousand badass criminals out on the streets again.'

'And they all owe us a favour,' Little Dog said. 'In our debt, see?'

Jake nodded. He saw alright. The Bandits' numbers were about to swell more than tenfold. With a thousand foot-soldiers, they could wreak some havoc.

'Ain't nobody stop us then,' he said.

Little Dog exhaled smoke towards the heavens. 'Aye,' he said. 'Ain't nobody.' He raised his fist in the air. 'Forever Bandits,' he said, meeting Jake's eye.

Jake raised his own fist, a kick of adrenaline running through him. 'Bandits forever,' he said.

49

The Honda smelled of old lady's perfume and pine air freshener and had a nodding dog stuck to the dashboard.

Gemma took the wheel and navigated her way from the farmhouse to a side road that ran up into Bombay. They reached the top of the hills and turned right, heading down towards the settlement itself – a school, a rugby club, and houses. No shops.

'Keep your eyes open,' she said, more to feel busy than because she thought Alex wouldn't. She was feeling jittery now and was anxious to get the last leg of their journey over with.

They dropped down through the settlement and headed towards the service centre at the motorway junction. Straight ahead took them towards Pukekohe, left towards the south and right towards Auckland. They passed a gas station, a fast food joint and another gas station as they went left and merged onto the motorway. There were no other motorists on the road, but a few cars were stopped at the side of the road.

Gemma dropped over the Bombay hills and took a left onto State Highway 2, heading east towards the Coromandel and the Bay of Plenty. It was quicker this way than continuing on down to Mercer, and she figured they were less likely to see anyone.

'You think they'll be home?' Alex asked suddenly.

Gemma frowned and looked at him. 'Of course,' she said.

'I just thought...you know...'

'No,' she said firmly. 'Mark said he'd be there, and that was always the plan, anyway.'

'The plan? You had a plan for this? Why am I not surprised?'

She saw he was smiling. 'Be prepared,' she said. 'The plan for any kind of disaster was always to get home, and for our family to come to us.'

'Because of safety in numbers?'

'Yeah, and our folks are older, too. We didn't want to leave them to fend for themselves if things went wrong.'

'Fair enough.' A pensive look crossed his face. 'I hope my Mum's okay.'

'I'm sure...'

'Oh shit.'

She followed his gaze to the wing mirror and saw the red and silver truck bearing down on them from behind. She cursed herself for getting distracted.

'Look out!'

They heard thuds as bullets struck the back of the car, and Gemma put her foot down. The turn-off was coming up fast and she stayed in the fast lane, hoping to throw them off. The speedo needle was hovering around one-forty and she doubted it would give her much more. More bullets hit the car and, at the last moment, she leaned hard left. The tyres screeched and protested and for a horrible moment she thought she was going to flip it. The Honda hung on though and she took the off-ramp with millimetres to spare. The Ford truck locked up behind them in a cloud of tyre smoke. Gemma raced down the off-ramp, round the small roundabout at the bottom and went right, cutting under the highway.

CURTIS WAS out of the truck and running to the side of the highway with the BAR before the truck had even stopped rocking on its shocks.

He threw the butt into his shoulder, seeing the white car emerge beneath him. He was certain it was them – they'd seen the car at a distance back in Bombay and chased it hard. Nobody else on the road – hadda be them. Dice had opened fire with his shotgun from the truck bed while they were still moving, surprising everyone by actually hitting the damn car. Now it was Curtis' turn and he was going to make the most of it.

He triggered the first shot through the roof of the car, saw it swerve, and fired again. As the car slowed to take a curve, he went for gold, emptying the magazine in seconds. The noise was ferocious and the recoil slammed his shoulder but he saw pieces flying off the vehicle and windows exploding before it disappeared from view behind some trees. He grinned to himself as he ran back towards the truck, waving at Dice. They had them now, he could feel it.

'You drive,' he shouted, deafened by the throaty boom of the big .308. 'And make sure you catch those fuckers.'

'HOLY SHIT,' Alex yelled, twisting in his seat to look behind them. 'You okay?'

Gemma nodded, concentrating on keeping the car on the road. They'd been showered with shards of glass when the windows went in, and the nodding dog on the windscreen had been blown away. At least he was the only casualty.

She had no idea how many rounds they'd taken but it had felt a bloody machine gun hammering at them.

'You okay?' Alex yelled again.

'Yes! Just make sure you shoot the bastards if you see them.'

'Here they come.'

She checked the mirrors. The truck was a few hundred metres back but coming fast. She estimated they were a couple of kilometres from home. Hopefully Mark would hear the shooting and come running. In some ways it seemed like madness to take this fight right to their door, but she knew that she and Alex couldn't outgun or outrun these people.

To stop now would be suicide. At least if they got close to home they'd have a fighting chance of getting out of it alive.

She checked the mirrors again. The truck had closed the gap further. She gassed the little Honda as much as she dared, throwing it down the country road, using the whole road to get through the twists and curves. She would never dare drive like this on a normal day, but today was not normal. Nor, she promised herself, would it be their last.

'Shoot back,' she said.

'It's too far,' Alex said, turning round to kneel on his seat. With the back windscreen blown out he could see clearly.

'Give the bastards something to think about,' she shouted.

He didn't argue, just fired a couple of shots. He couldn't see where they went and the truck didn't stop. If anything, it accelerated.

'Keep going,' Gemma shouted over the howl of the wind through the car. 'We're nearly there.'

She could see the turn into their road coming up. They were nearly home.

50

The whine of a car being wrung out carried across the fields and my head snapped up before I'd even registered what the sound was. It was mixed with the roar of a gruntier engine, and even over the two engines I could hear the pop of shots.

I grabbed Archie's hand and we were off and running, Jethro bounding along as if it were a game.

'What's going on Dad?' Archie wanted to know. We reached the gate and I bundled him through, securing it behind us.

'Inside,' I said, ignoring the question. 'Rob!' I shouted towards the house. 'You guys, out here, quick!'

I got Archie into the sleepout and unslung the Rossi. 'Stay here,' I told him.

The three older folk came hurrying across from the house, Rob with his Lee Enfield in his hands. The engines were getting louder in the background and I could hear more shooting.

'What the hell's going on?' Rob said.

'I don't know, but I'm going to find out. You guys stay in here and stay down. Anyone tries to get in, shoot them.'

I shooed Jethro inside and shut the door behind him, then set off at a run down the drive. It sounded like a real gunfight and the engines were definitely coming towards us. One of the guns shooting was a big semi-auto, maybe a .308 or .30-06.

I reached the end of the driveway as a white Honda came screeching round the corner, the tail sliding out. It fishtailed, corrected and gassed it towards me. Close behind it was a big red and silver truck. I could see a figure standing in the back, shooting over the roof of the cab. Fortunately for whoever was in the fleeing Honda the truck was bouncing and swerving all over the place.

I hunkered down by the fence with the Rossi aimed over the top, sighting on the Honda as it flew towards me. It jinked a couple of times, making it hard to sight in, but I caught a glimpse of the driver. I focussed hard, not quite believing it.

Gemma was in the driving seat, her hands taut on the wheel. She was looking towards me in between checking the mirrors. In the front passenger seat was a guy I didn't recognise.

I shifted my focus to the truck, seeing a huge man behind the wheel. Beside him was a skinny girl who was hanging out the passenger window, firing a short-barrelled weapon at the Honda. Leaning over the top of the cab was another big guy and the weapon he had looked like a magazine-fed automatic rifle. He was still firing and now I could see that the Honda had definitely taken some hits.

'Son of a bitch,' I muttered.

I sighted in on the driver and put a round into the windscreen. It careened off without shattering the glass, and the guy didn't even flinch. The Honda was nearly up to me. I worked the lever and put another round into the windscreen. The guy noticed this time and flinched slightly.

I worked the lever, shifted aim slightly and blew the wing mirror off in front of the girl. She pulled back inside and the guy hit the brakes. The guy in the back was thrown forward and nearly lost his weapon – I could hear him cursing from where I was – and Gemma braked hard. She overshot our driveway and went into a skid, smoke pouring off the tyres.

Turning back towards the truck, I saw that it was coming to a stop

about thirty metres away from me. Three baddies and an auto rifle –
way too close for comfort. I needed to even the odds.

The scope wasn't necessary at this range; instinct and experience
took over.

I worked the lever, took a quick bead on the girl who was opening
the passenger door with a submachine gun of some sort in her hands,
and pumped a round through the open window. She took the hit in
the chest and was thrown back against the pillar, her weapon
discharging into the air in a fast burst.

Lever, shift. The guy in the back was steadying himself but didn't
have his weapon up yet. I moved again, cracking the windscreen with
my next shot. I wasn't sure if I'd hit him or not but the man mountain
rolled out the driver's door and dropped from my sight.

More shooting sounded from my left and I glanced that way.
Gemma and the guy had bailed out of the Honda, which was slewed
across the road past our gate. They were tucked down behind it,
Gemma firing a pistol over the bonnet, the guy a rifle, both pumping
rounds towards the truck.

As I turned my attention back, the big rifle opened up and I was
taking fire. A chunk was blown out of the fence beside me, another
round cracked past my shoulder and I threw myself sideways to the
ground. The rifle was deafeningly loud so close up. Bullets continued
cracking my way as I rolled and got on my belly, getting the Rossi into
my shoulder. In a split second, the world around me ceased to exist
and it was just me and him.

I could see the guy clearly, standing up in the tray of the truck
with the big rifle at his shoulder, pumping rounds my way. I could see
the puffs of smoke, the recoil into his body, even some of the ejected
shells spinning through the air. I stared down the barrel at him for
what seemed like a long moment before the thump of a bullet into
the fence railing above snapped me back into reality.

My finger curled around the trigger and I squeezed through. A
miss. Lever, aim. Another miss. Lever, aim. My last round knocked
one of his legs out and he fell awkwardly in the tray. I rolled to the
side further and snatched a handful of shells from a pouch,

thumping them into the tube as fast as I could, dropping a couple in the dirt. It occurred to me that a selective fire weapon would be very handy.

I could hear more shooting from the direction of the Honda, and a shotgun from the truck, presumably the huge man. I crawled under the fence into the paddock, scrambled up and ran doubled over along the fence line towards the road.

51

The volume of fire was incredible and Rob knew that Mark was in the shit. 'I'm going out to help him,' he said, and Sandy grabbed his arm.

'No, you can't go out there,' she said, desperation in her voice. 'Please.'

'He needs my help.' He started for the door, but she held onto his arm.

'Rob, please. What about...' She indicated with her head towards Archie, who was huddled against Jenny, his eyes like saucers.

Rob frowned, torn. The gunfire continued outside.

'What about upstairs, Poppa?' Archie said. 'Dad said you can shoot from up there.'

Rob's gaze shifted to the ladder up into the man-hole, and he nodded. 'I'll go up and have a look,' he said.

Sandy let him go and he carefully clambered up the ladder with his rifle. He stepped over to the hatch and realised Archie had made a good call. There was an excellent view of the front of the property. He could clearly see a white car across the road to the left and two people shooting from behind it towards a red and silver ute to the right.

There was a body on the ground beside the ute, a man crouched in the back of it with a rifle beside what looked like a bundled tarpaulin, and Mark lying down on the driveway behind the fence. He grabbed up the binoculars hanging on a nail by the hatch, and scanned the scene. He could see Mark loading his rifle then saw him crawl under the fence into the paddock.

There looked to be someone else on the far side of the ute and he could see puffs of smoke as that person fired. The two behind the white car, also mostly out of sight to Rob, were trading shots with him.

Rob scanned back past the ute and saw Bevan creeping his way down the shoulder of the road towards the scene. He was still some distance away. The binos moved back to the ute and he saw the man – a big, thug-looking man – clumsily trying to stand. Mark didn't seem to have seen him, but the guy still had the rifle in his hands.

Putting the binos down, Rob chambered a round in the Lee Enfield and slid the barrel through the hatch. He settled himself, sighting down the iron sights and taking a bead on the man in the back of the ute. He wished he had a scope, as his eyesight was not great at this distance.

I GOT HALFWAY down the paddock when I saw the guy rise up from the bed of the truck.

The big rifle was pointing at me and he fired even as he was coming up. I dropped to a knee and fired, levered, fired, levered and fired again. The big rifle boomed again and again and I got a decent bead on his torso as he got painfully to his feet. Just as I squeezed the trigger a round took him fair in the face and I saw the contents of his head eject out the back in a red spray.

He dropped like a stone, tumbling over the side of the truck. I spun and looked behind me, not knowing where the shot had come from. My eyes settled on the hatch below the roofline of the sleep out, and the barrel poking out.

Rob had my back.

I turned and continued forward, sliding rounds into the tube as I went. The shotgun was still shooting from the other side of the ute. I could see the girl I'd shot, motionless on the ground beside the open passenger door. I got right up to the roadside fence, only a few metres away from the truck.

IN THE SLEEPOUT, Jenny, Sandy and Archie could hear occasional bullets pinging off and punching into the building.

They were directly in the line of fire from the road, but the reinforcing that Mark had put in place kept them safe. All the same, they huddled together on the floor, keeping their heads down and praying for it to end soon. Jenny looked at the shotgun leaning against the wall, and crawled over to get it. Another bullet hit the wall somewhere behind her and she dragged the gun back to her position.

She held it across her knees and hoped she wouldn't have to use it again. But, hunched down beside Sandy with Archie between them, she knew she would do whatever she needed to do.

Nobody would be coming through that door to harm her grandson.

GEMMA SAW the man from back of the ute tumble over the side and land on the road behind the man mountain who had been driving.

He was too busy trying to kill her and Alex to notice. She fired another two rounds, saw the slide lock open on the Glock and she dropped down behind the car again. She ejected the empty magazine and slid in her last full one, thumbing down the slide release and letting the slide run forward.

Beside her, Alex ducked down too, fumbling with the Marlin. He'd already changed magazines once but he wasn't confident with it. She peeked over the bonnet and saw the huge man still crouched down beside the driver's door, his shotgun pointing towards them. She ducked again and the shotgun boomed, this time blowing out a window on the far side of the Honda.

'Jesus,' she muttered, barely able to hear herself over the shooting. If things didn't turn around fast, they were toast. She could hear firing from over near the gate, and guessed it was Mark. She hadn't wanted to bring the fight home, but she knew that if anyone was going to bail them out of the shit, it would be him.

'Got it,' Alex said, satisfied as he worked the bolt and chambered a fresh round in the Marlin.

The car rocked with another hit, and Gemma didn't dare raise her head above the bonnet. 'Wait,' she said, crouching with the Glock ready in both hands.

The shotgun boomed, the Honda rocked and she pushed up, punching the Glock out in a double-handed grip, Alex coming up beside her with the Marlin at his shoulder. The huge man was pumping the slide on his shotgun and looking their way, and she could see his eyes go wide as he realised they'd outsmarted him.

The Glock kicked in her hands as she squeezed the trigger and kept on squeezing it. The Marlin was cracking beside her and she saw the man taking hits. His body shuddered with the impacts – she didn't know if it was her or Alex hitting him, but it didn't matter – and he fell back on his butt. He still tried to bring the shotgun on line but both of them kept firing and he took more hits. Gemma saw blood spurt from the side of his head and he twisted, slumping backwards, the shotgun falling from his grasp.

Alex fired again and Gemma lowered her pistol. 'Stop,' she said, 'he's down.'

She saw her husband then, in the paddock at the roadside fence, leaning his rifle against the fence railings and drawing a pistol from his belt.

He started to climb the fence railings.

52

I was almost over the fence when the girl on the ground suddenly sat bolt upright.

Her left shoulder was a mess of blood and meat and her face was streaked with it.

She was barely five metres from me and I could see the craziness in her eyes. The submachine gun was still in her right hand and she was bringing it up. The muzzle was level with me before I even registered and she fired, the bullets zinging past my head. I flinched and punched out the Ruger in my right hand, firing by instinct, three rounds in quick succession, her body shuddering as the rounds all hit home.

The submachine gun triggered another burst as the barrel dropped and I heard the rounds impacting the fence railings below me. I fired two more rounds into her torso, lifted the barrel slightly, and drilled the last round through her nose. The body slumped sideways and the submachine gun dropped. I jumped back down and shoved the empty Ruger into the holster, grabbing my Rossi again. I quickly scaled the fence and moved around the ute. The girl was clearly dead, her head leaking fluids onto the asphalt of the road.

The big man that Rob had dropped was in a heap on the road,

also leaking blood from his head. There was a big hole in his fore-head and his sightless eyes were staring at the sky. Beside him was a massive guy, flat on his back with a shotgun beside him. His front was wet with blood and I could see multiple holes in his torso. If I was a betting man, I'd say that Gemma and the guy with her had shot him.

I moved to the cab and confirmed it was clear, then checked the rear of the ute. I yanked aside the bundled tarpaulin and saw the body of a woman there. Chubby, dyed hair, and with stab wounds in her chest. Dead.

There were more weapons beside her too, and boxes of ammunition.

I stepped back, sucking in a breath. My heart was already pounding with adrenaline, and it skipped a beat when I saw Gemma running towards me. I put down my rifle and moved past the dead bodies and opened my arms. She crashed into me so hard I staggered and I wrapped her up tight, lifting her off the ground as she cried. She cried hard and I felt my own eyes leaking too, not quite believing she was actually home and alive. She was beaten and bloodied but she was *alive*.

We held each other for what seemed like forever until Gemma let go and wiped her eyes. We laughed at each other and I wiped tears from her face then kissed her firmly on the mouth.

'I can't believe you're here,' I said. 'Who the hell are these guys?'

'Long story.' She turned to the guy who was standing off, waiting awkwardly. 'Alex, this is Mark,' she said.

He came over and we shook hands.

'Alex is from work,' she said. 'He's been with me since this all happened. We've pretty much walked from work.'

'We were getting a bit anxious,' I said, then a thought suddenly hit me. 'Is it just these pricks or are there more to come?'

'Just them,' Alex said, and I nodded.

'Good. There's been enough shit going on here this week.'

'Is Archie okay? Where is he?' Gemma rubbed her face and ran a hand through her hair. 'What about Mum and Dad? Who's here?'

'They're all here and they're all okay.' I realised that, despite the carnage around us, I was grinning like an idiot. 'Shit, I can't believe you're here. I can't believe you made it.'

My wife gave her companion a sideways look. 'We nearly didn't,' she said. 'It's pretty rough out there. Man, there's riots and everything, we had...' She shook her head and looked away. 'It's pretty bad,' she said quietly.

I heard footsteps behind us and turned to see Bevan arrive, his AR-15 at the ready.

'Holy fuckin' shit,' he said. 'Who the fuck are these guys?' He noticed Gemma then and raised a hand in greeting. 'Hey, Gemma.' He stuck his hand out and shook with Alex. 'You guys all okay?'

'Yep.' I was about to pull Gemma in again but we both heard the shouting from our driveway as Archie came running.

'Mum! Mum! Mummy!'

She ran to him and they were both crying by the time they met and she swept him up in her arms and they clung to each other.

I didn't want my son to see the bodies and the mess, so I gently guided them up the driveway and told Gemma I would be there soon. I went back to where Alex and Bevan stood together, Bevan checking out the carbine that Alex was holding.

'Where'd you get that from, mate?' Bevan was saying.

'Um, from a guy,' Alex said uncomfortably.

'You bought it?'

'Um, no...we took it from him...'

Bevan was about to ask another question but I intervened, seeing how uncomfortable Alex was with the conversation. The other neighbours were coming down the road too, some armed, most not.

'Guys, we need to get this shit off the road.' I jerked a thumb at the ute and the bodies, and the shot-to-shit Honda. 'There's a dead woman in the back of the ute too, and some guns. Give me a hand and we'll get the bodies into the back of it and move it off the road.'

Between us we got the girl and the big man into the back, the other neighbours standing back and watching. When it came time to move the massive guy, I called on a couple of the neighbours to help. They did so, gingerly trying to help us lift him before I got grumpy.

'Come on, get into it,' I snapped. 'I'm not breaking my back for this fat fucker. Put some effort in.'

We got him up onto the back of the ute and shuffled him up, closing the tailgate after him. I pulled the tarp off the dead woman and spread it across all four bodies.

'Bevan, can you take this to your place mate?' He looked reluctant and I raised my eyebrows expectantly. 'Kids don't need to see this shit mate. We'll sort it out later, okay?'

'I don't want them there for too long,' he said, but he did as I asked and moved the truck down the road.

'You two,' I said to the two guys who had helped us with the bodies, recognising one as one of the Macklins' workers, 'go and get some water and brooms and wash the blood and shit off the road, okay?'

They went off to do it, and I got Alex to help me push the Honda to the side of the road. The keys were in it but there was glass everywhere inside and I didn't fancy getting cut.

By the time Alex and I got back up to the house things had calmed down and a pot of water was on the boil. Nothing like a cup of tea in times of high emotion. Archie and Gemma were on the couch together, and it was clear that he wasn't going to be letting her go any time soon.

I introduced Alex to everyone and Gemma explained that he had walked with her all the way from Freemans Bay. I knew there would be more details to that journey but she was careful not to go there while Archie was listening. Rob took me aside and asked if he had hit the guy with the BAR. I told him he had and he nodded slowly, processing that. I knew it wasn't sitting comfortably with him, all the violence of the last few days, even though he was stepping up and doing what needed to be done.

'You saved my arse,' I told him. 'That guy would have dropped me. That was a hell of a shot.'

He nodded, taking some solace from that, and I shook his hand. 'It was the turning point, dropping that guy.'

'I'm just glad you're okay,' he said quietly. 'And my girl's home safely.'

After washing up, I fetched a bottle of bourbon from the cupboard and cracked it open. I poured us all a decent slug and we toasted the safe homecoming of Gemma and our new friend Alex. He seemed overwhelmed by everything that was going on, but Sandy took him under her wing and got him busy helping her in the kitchen.

53

As darkness fell, Rob and I walked down to Bevan's.

The red and silver ute was parked outside his shed, and we found him in the garage. He had unloaded the weapons from the back of it, and had them laid out on the floor with their magazines and spare ammo. He looked up as we came in, and I could see the excitement in his face. He was loving having all these guns in his hands.

'Alright mate?' I said, casting an eye over them.

'There's some really good shit here,' he enthused. 'Look at this; a fuckin' BAR. That shit is fuckin' brutal.'

He was right; it was fuckin' brutal. So brutal it had nearly killed me, Gemma and Alex.

'You're not wrong,' I agreed. I checked the weapons again. 'Where's that M3?'

He looked around as if he had no idea, and spread his hands. 'Um, I'm not sure...'

'Come on, where is it?' I fixed him with a glare. 'You can't help yourself, Bevan. This is not all for you to lay claim on.'

He looked surprised. 'Oh come on, Mark, these arseholes came to my home...'

'No, they came to my home,' I corrected him. 'Trying to kill my wife.'

'That was a helluva big shootout,' he said. 'They could've killed any of us.'

'Not you,' Rob retorted sharply. 'You dropped your nuts and hung back while him and my daughter dealt with it.'

Bevan looked like he'd been slapped. 'I didn't drop...'

'And he popped one of the fuckers from a hundred metres away on iron sights,' I said, jerking a thumb towards Rob. 'Saved my life.'

Bevan stewed on it for a moment. 'You can't say I dropped my nuts, because I didn't. I had to get my gear and get down there, and there was bullets flying everywhere. I couldn't just run down the middle of the road; I'd've got shot. I got there as fast as I could.'

I let my anger simmer a bit, and took a breath before speaking. 'Look, whichever way you cut it, you have no claim to keep all these. You've got a shitload of weapons of your own.'

'I want the SKS,' he said obstinately. 'It's a real Russian-made one.'

'No,' I said. 'Get me the M3 and we'll take the rest of this stuff. We'll keep some and I'll give some to the neighbours.'

We eyeballed each other for a few seconds before he backed down. He fetched the British submachine gun from inside, along with the four magazines for it. I put it with the other weapons and led the other two men outside.

'You got access to the Macklins' little digger?' I asked.

Bevan nodded. 'I can get it.'

'Go get it now, and we'll bury these fuckers.'

'What about the truck? And the other car?'

'I've got an idea for them, but one thing at a time.'

We waited while he headed off over to the Macklins' place, and I took the opportunity to quickly check inside his house. I didn't trust him not to have nicked anything else, and I was right. He had kept back a few boxes of 9mm Parabellum ammo, stacked on his dining table where I guessed he had put the M3. As far as I knew he didn't have any 9mm-calibre weapons.

I took them back out to the garage. Rob rolled his eyes when I showed him – he was getting a serious dislike for Bevan.

The digger was old but functional, and I got Bevan to drive it into the paddock beside his house, over into the far corner.

'Why my place?' he wanted to know.

'Because I don't want my wife and son to have a constant reminder of how close they came to being killed at home,' I said bluntly. 'Just dig the fuckin' hole.'

He did as he was told, scowling all the way, and I fumed as I watched him. I was physically and mentally drained, and I didn't need his shit. Our fragile relationship was under strain but right at that moment I didn't give a shit. I just wanted to bury these pricks and get on with it.

Once the hole was deep enough I drove the Ford over and we dumped the bodies in the hole. Bevan covered it again, smoothing out the ground as best he could. There were no tears shed, no sadness. I was tempted to spit on their graves but held back. Those pieces of shit deserved nothing from me, not even my spit.

I drove the ute back to Bevan's house, thanked him, and loaded the weapons and ammo into it. He was still grumpy when we left.

Rob and I went home and unloaded all the weapons and ammo into the garage – I didn't trust Bevan not to come foraging, so put them under lock and key. While Rob went inside I looked over the weapons again, deciding what I wanted to keep.

The BAR was a given. A semi-auto .308 with a 20-round magazine would be very handy when you needed to reach out and touch someone.

The Norinco CQ 5.56 was a Chinese semi-auto version of the M16 in .223. This one had half a dozen 30-round mags with it. The pump action shotgun the massive man had been using was a Winchester SXP with a 28-inch barrel and a 4-round tube capacity. The M3 was an interesting weapon. It was a ruggedly ugly little 9mm submachine gun. It had a simple telescopic butt and a 30-round magazine.

The Beretta 1301 Tactical shotgun was the Marine model in black and silver, and would be very handy.

The last one was an SKS carbine in 7.62x39mm, the old Russian calibre. It was also a semi-auto, fed with 10-round stripper clips, of which there were several. I put that aside as one that I was happy to give away. The ammo wasn't common and I figured we could live without it. I added the Winchester to it and kept the rest aside. I knew I was keeping the best weapons, but what the hell, I figured we had earned it. My family were pretty much the only ones dealing with the threats we faced, and we needed to be equipped to do so.

I added the 7mm Magnum Ruger M77 I had taken from the shit-birds at Meremere to the giveaway pile, plus the bolt action Norinco .22 recovered from the thief my mother had shot. I nodded, satisfied. Four weapons to share out with the neighbours, four for us.

By the time I had cleaned up again and gone inside, living arrangements had been worked out. One of the camp stretchers had been put up and Alex would sleep in the lounge, meaning nobody else had to move. If it was to be a longer term situation that would readdressed later, but for now, he was just happy to be sleeping inside.

Dinner was soon ready and we all sat at the dining table together to eat. Sandy, Jenny and Alex had been busy and we had rice risotto with chicken and vegetables from the garden. Gemma sat between Archie and I and I felt like a goofy teenager again now that she was home. I hadn't realised how stressful it had been not knowing where she was or whether she was safe, not until I actually had her home.

Looking around the candle-lit table, I knew that even though our house was now home to a collection of people who otherwise would never have been together, it was okay. We were safe and warm, we were fed and watered, and we were together.

In the days ahead, and with the trouble that came, together we were going to need to stand fast.

END

The **Early Warning** series continues with *Stand Fast*,
the third book in the series.

BONUS CHAPTERS

EARLY WARNING SERIES #3
STAND FAST

It had been four days since things turned to shit, and a lot had changed.

Instead of just our family of three living the quiet life on our small property in rural North Waikato, we also now had three grandparents and a work colleague living with us. We were surrounded by people who were poorly prepared for such an event. Thieves and thugs were roaming the countryside, taking what they could get and killing indiscriminately. Martial law had been imposed and the military were deployed to the streets.

It had been four days since I'd seen my wife, Gemma, until she and her workmate Alex turned up home in a hail of bullets, pursued by a family of psychos they had crossed paths with. That had been yet another gunfight, this time practically on our doorstep. I'd lost count of how many people I'd killed in the last four days. How many my father-in-law Rob had killed. Christ, even my own mother, Jenny, had gunned down a lowlife who had shot at my son and tried to rob our place.

Even in years as a street cop, I'd never seen carnage like this, especially not in such a short space of time. People had gone mad. Ever since a giant earthquake, probably the biggest the country had ever seen, had knocked out Wellington and forced the Prime Minister to declare a national state of emergency, people had just lost their shit.

My family was prepared for a natural disaster, but even we were not fully ready for what hit us. Most people were caught completely unawares, and it showed.

As the early morning sunlight broke through a crack in the curtains, I watched Gemma sleeping. She'd been on the road with Alex the last four days, walking from central Auckland to get home. She'd told me some of the story last night as we sat in the darkness, sipping whiskey and regrouping.

She had talked and cried as she finally started to process it all, and to let go of the stress she'd been under. Alex had chipped in as well, and his respect for her was obvious. He told us numerous times that he wouldn't have made it without her.

They'd dodged crooks, been forced to kill on multiple occasions to defend themselves, and braved the elements and the people they'd come across. It had been a hell of an adventure, if you could call it that, and certainly nothing she had ever contemplated happening.

Gemma was a normal woman, working part-time in an office, running around after me and our 7-year old son Archie, keeping an eye on her elderly parents. Keeping the wheels turning. But she was tough, tougher than she had ever realised, and it was her mental strength and determination that had ultimately got them home.

It had taken a long time for things to settle down yesterday. Archie was excited to see his Mum again, and her parents, Rob and Sandy, had been incredibly relieved too. Even my own mother, never a great fan of her daughter-in-law, had been glad to see her. Gemma and Alex had both taken the opportunity to have a proper wash with hot water and soap, to wash their hair, brush their teeth and put on clean clothes. I had loaned some clothes to Alex, who only had what he had carried. My clothes were baggy on him but they would do.

Gemma had stayed on Archie's bed until he went to sleep.

Even though we'd been up late I'd been awake since before dawn, as had become my habit. I had quietly patrolled the house and checked outside, but nothing seemed disturbed. Fully clothed, I'd sat back on the bed and watched over Gemma as she slept.

She twitched in her sleep and had woken during the night, reaching out for me, wanting the comfort of knowing I was there. She was battered from her ordeal, physically and emotionally. A graze on her cheek was healing and would soon fade. We had iced her ribs and back where she'd been booted, and anti-inflammatories would help sort that out soon enough.

I sat in the dim grey light, listening to her breathing. Keeping watch.

I couldn't quite believe she was home.

THE DIVISION SERIES #1

SMOKE AND MIRRORS

Baghdad, Iraq
  Two years ago

It wasn't called the Highway to Hell for nothing.

Driving on the highway from the city to Baghdad International Airport was like 200 miles of dodgems, only every dodgem potentially carried a bomb or a carload of ruthless bastards who wanted to slice off your head on Al-Jazheera and drag your corpse through the streets.

Archer loved it and loathed it at the same time; the thrill of the risk was intoxicating, but the reality of it going bad was too terrifying to contemplate. In his team of PMCs they had a deal-last man standing finished any wounded then took one himself.

Deny the pricks the pleasure of doing it themselves.

His team, he thought to himself. For about another hour, they were still his team. After that he was on a big bird to LA to meet up with a tidy American Army Major, to spend 3 weeks eating, drinking and screwing, in no particular order. After 3 weeks R&R he was coming back, and they'd be his team again.

He cast a lazy eye to the driver on his right, big Grunter, a bald former SWAT team officer in Johannesburg. He was built like a house and ate constantly when he wasn't working out. He had seen more action in Jo'burg than most squaddies in Iraq. He drove the Nissan Patrol like it was a Tonka toy.

Behind Grunter sat Jacko, a former Para sergeant who had served a full 20 years and gone straight into the private sector to earn his pension. The Brit was a tattooed chain smoker and notorious practical-joker. Archer's boxers still scratched from when Jacko had drowned them in starch and turned them to cardboard.

In the rear of the wagon was the gunner, on this occasion Bula, the Fijian alcoholic who had served with 22 SAS for a decade before going private. Constantly smiling and hung over he was nearly fifty and the veteran of a dozen wars around the globe.

Archer kept his eyes moving, scanning his arc to the left, the barrel of his Russian AK-47 resting on his left knee, finger alongside the trigger guard, stock folded for ease of movement. Vehicles all around them, moving like people on a conveyer belt, an endless stream towards the airport and its surrounds. Iraqis stared back at the white faces with either indifference or open disdain and hostility. Not fear. These people were not afraid of the heavily armed men in the packet, identical in their polo shirts and wrap around shades. Men like this had come and gone, and would always do so, and it meant nothing. They meant nothing; just another white face.

The sun was at a dangerous angle, and Grunter was squinting behind his shades and the sun visor. The white Renault in front of them carried their other team members and their clients, a pair of oil company execs who had spent a week schmoozing and were on their way home. Archer was accompanying them, which suited the team because they could tie in the drop-off with picking up a new team member on his way in from the UK. Dusty, up front with his fellow former Royal Marine, Tim, would be running the team in Archer's absence. He was a good man but probably a little more conservative than Archer would have liked. Although conservative wasn't always a bad thing in this part of the world.

Dusty was giving the constant commentary that they could hear over their earpieces, identifying any risks or potential trouble spots as they came into range.

'White truck, right, 150. Man in back with AK. 100 now, not aware. Closing up, still not aware...'

Bula's voice came over the radio then.

'Hey, red Beamer coming from behind, left of us, 3 or 4 boys. Unfriendlies, keeping eyes.'

Archer caught sight in the wing mirror of the BMW coming up on the left, two boys in the front and at least another in the back. All of them had eyes on the Patrol, and he could see the tension in their bodies.

At the same time, Dusty came back on.

'Dead dog, right, 100.'

IED, thought Archer, thumbing off his safety catch at the same time.

'Drop back Grunter,' he ordered and felt the Patrol slow immediately, 'eyes up guys. I've got the left, keep your arcs.'

The red BMW was almost even with them now and he could see two in the back now. The angle was no good for seeing weapons though. He rested his finger lightly on the trigger and kept one eye on the car and one on the rest of the surrounds. The gap between the Patrol and the Renault had opened up slightly, allowing them more room to move in an IA.

Archer saw a flicker of movement from the back seat as the closest passenger lifted the barrel of an AK into view. All eyes from the car were on his now in his wing mirror and he knew it was game on.

'Grunter, hit it!' he barked, the AK coming into view properly as the window came down. He raised his own AK as Grunter jerked the wheel left and smashed into the front wing of the Beamer.

Archer triggered a burst through the window straight into the interior of the car as it lurched to the left, at the same time as an almighty explosion erupted from the right, strong enough to rock the Patrol and blow out windows in the cars around it. The windscreen shattered under the force of debris and Archer felt stings across his face and arm.

Traffic closed up all around them as cars crashed into each other, and Grunter jerked the wheel left again, smashing into a beaten up pick up that had drifted in front of him. He gunned the big engine and shoved the pick up out of the way, clearing a space to get to the shoulder of the road. The white Renault was also moving left, seeking a way clear of the carnage.

Archer saw the BMW coming back, accelerating up on the left, openly displaying AKs out the windows now.

'Contact left! Contact left!' he barked into his mouthpiece, one hand depressing the pressel switch on his chest and the other levelling the AK. He cut loose another burst, longer this time, raking the windscreen of the BMW to blind the driver. Jacko had slid across the backseat and opened up too, a long burst into the back which took out the closest passenger.

Too late, he realised they had made the wrong move, both vehicles coming to the left.

A second explosion detonated on the shoulder of the road, bigger than the first and almost directly in front of the Renault. The front of the car lifted off the ground in a shower of dust and dirt and flame, crashing back down at an angle and almost rolling, rocking on its springs as it settled back down again at the edge of a smoking crater.

Grunter was blinded and ran straight into the back of the Renault, shunting it forward before he managed to stop.

Surrounded by a dust cloud and with screams in his ears, Archer shouted, 'Debus, debus! IA!'

He threw the door open and leaped out, snapping open the butt stock of the AK and shouldering it, seeking targets.

The boys in the BMW knew they were there and would be using the Patrol as a start point, so they needed to get clear quickly, secure the guys from the Renault, and move.

Archer moved forward as per their IA drills, bellowing, 'Moving!' and making a magazine change on the run.

He got to the wreck of the Renault and wrenched open the left rear door. He could see immediately that the two execs were shaken and scratched but okay. Dusty was bleeding in the front passenger's seat, the front of his armour saturated from a wound in his face. Tim was dead, most of his head gone and sprayed across the execs in the back.

Archer seized the closest client by the arm and yanked him out, shouting, 'Move! Move now!'

Gunfire sounded behind him above the heavy buzz in his ears but he ignored it, focussing on the task at hand. The exec tumbled out and Archer pushed him to the ground a couple of metres away with an order to stay down. The second one was frozen and wouldn't budge. Archer grabbed him by the collar and jerked him across the back seat but he locked his arms and legs against the door frame and began wailing like a scared child.

Not breaking stride, Archer thumped him in the face with a left jab and stunned him, then yanked him out and pushed him down beside his mate. Kneeling over them he scanned around, seeing the BMW pulled up near the Patrol, all doors open and fire coming from behind it. Jacko and Grunter were deployed at each end of the Patrol, trading shots with the Beamer boys. Bula was cutting around another vehicle, the RPK in his hands looking like a .22 to a normal sized man. He was seeking an angle to out flank the enemy.

Archer slapped both execs on the head and shouted at them to stay down, then pushed up and returned to the Renault. The front passenger door was buckled and wouldn't open. He used his rifle barrel to clear the broken glass and reached in to Dusty. The former Marine was barely conscious, bleeding heavily from a nasty gouge to his left cheek and another slice across his forehead. His nose looked broken, and Archer realised he had probably smashed his face into the dash. A quick check revealed no other obvious injuries.

'Come on you whinging fucken Pom!'

Archer slung his AK and grabbed his mate under the arms, heaving him up and dragging him through the window. He dragged him across to the execs and lay him down. Ripping Dusty's own field dressing from his webbing Archer pressed it against the cheek wound and used his arm to wipe some of the blood away. He ripped a length of duct tape from his own webbing and secured it across the dressing and half way round Dusty's head.

He checked the lads again and saw Bula had got distracted. Somebody had opened up from the far side of the road at him, and he had now taken a knee behind a vehicle and was trying to pick off the target through the wreckage around him.

Archer moved right, keeping well clear of his own lads' arcs, AK in the shoulder. He could see two of the Beamer boys behind the engine block, each with an AK, taking turns to rise and pop a short burst at Jacko and Grunter.

Archer dropped flat on his belly and took aim. He could see the side of one of the boys around the edge of the wrecked BMW, and let loose a quick double tap. A scream sounded and the gunman fell backwards into full view. Archer gave him a longer burst that shook him like a bad disco dancer and he dropped his AK, writhing in the dirt. His mate wasn't stupid though and kept his position behind the engine block, his feet hidden by the wheel.

Archer saw his gun barrel poke up above the bonnet of the BMW and readied himself. The gun edged up horizontally and loosed off a spray of rounds blindly, the bullets sweeping across the side of the Patrol and punching more holes in it.

Jacko was closest to Archer and returned a burst of his own, before yelling, 'Stoppage!'

Archer saw him ripping his magazine off and slapping in a new one, then yanking at the bolt.

'Stoppage!' he shouted again, indicating a jam.

The other Beamer boy obviously understood some English because he saw his opportunity to seal the deal. Archer rose at the same time as the insurgent and double tapped him in the chest. The Iraqi fell back behind the car, his AK firing wildly into the sky.

'Moving!'

Archer moved forward and right, seeing the three Iraqis behind the car. One dead on his back, the second rolling on his side with the AK still in his hand, trying to bring it round, the third at the back trading shots with Grunter.

He put a burst into the wounded gunman, the third oblivious to his presence, and moved in closer. The third gunman saw him now and swung round to meet the new threat, but too late. As he moved, Grunter took his head off at the shoulders with a triple burst, and Archer caught him in the front as he went down.

Archer put another burst into the head of the first man, and repeated it on the second. Grunter had moved forward now and finished off what was left of his own target.

More gunfire sounded from the roadway, a couple of single AK shots then a sustained burst of machine gun fire.

Bula came back through the dust at a jog, the RPK in his hands and blood dribbling from his leg. He was still grinning.

'Got 'im bro,' he shouted, taking a knee near Jacko, covering arcs again.

'Grunter, get the wagon going,' Archer ordered, 'Jacko with me. Bula; with Grunter.'

They moved quickly, Jacko covering the growing crowd of onlookers as Archer got to the execs and Dusty.

He took a knee over them and covered an arc, hearing horn blasts and roaring Humvee engines as an American PMC team approached from the rear. There were smashing sounds as the column forced its way through the traffic, even though it would have been easier to go wide into the desert.

Not much difference between some of the PMCs and their service comrades, Archer thought.

Grunter got the Patrol going and manoeuvred fully onto the shoulder, Bula trotting behind him as he made his way forward. They quickly loaded the execs into the backseat and onto the floor, Jacko over them.

Archer got Dusty into the back as well then moved back to the Renault. Bula got a Union Jack out and slung it across the back of the Patrol to face the Yanks when they arrived. The last thing they wanted now was friendly fire.

Tim's legs were stuck under the steering wheel and Archer was working at freeing them, trying to ignore the sticky mess around him, when he heard the Yank packet arrive. He got the right leg free and got Tim half out the window when he heard a burst of fire.

Cradling Tim in his arms he threw a glance over his shoulder, instinct telling him this was going bad.

A Humvee was pulled up near the Patrol, and a gunner was leaning out the window with his M4, shouting at Bula who stood near the back of the Patrol with his RPK.

'Oh shit...'

Archer let Tim down and started to move back to his team, waving and shouting at the soldier, but it was too late.

The gunner was obviously amped up and used to giving orders that were obeyed. Bula was also amped up but still in control, but that wasn't the problem. He was holding a machine gun and had dark skin, and even though Archer clearly understood he was shouting 'Security patrol! We're on your side!' the young Yank obviously couldn't understand a Fijian accent.

The M4 burst off rounds and Bula went down.

'Fuck!'

Archer sprinted forward now, hands in the air, shouting, 'Cease fire! Cease fire!'

He got to the roadway and the Humvee emptied out. The gunslinger who had shot Bula darted towards him with his carbine raised, ready to finish him, convinced he had taken a Taleban down.

'Stand down you fucken moron!' Jacko bellowed at him, debussing with Grunter, both of them wise enough to leave their AKs behind.

The gunner swung his rifle towards them then paused as the two white men confronted him. His gaze went back to where Bula lay still in the dust.

'What the hell...'

He never finished his sentence because Grunter seized him by the throat with one big mitt and stripped him of his weapon with the other. He lifted the other guy onto his tip-toes and tossed the carbine aside.

Jacko went to Bula and Archer reached them just as the vehicle commander, a young surfer looking dude, pointed a rifle at Grunter's head.

'Stand down, boy,' he drawled, calm and quiet. 'Do it now.'

Grunter tossed the gunner aside like a rag doll and stepped back, hands raised and his face as impassive as ever. Jacko stood and came over. He had blood on his hands and rage in his eyes.

'He's dead,' he said flatly. He raised his hands to shoulder height, showing the blood on his hands to the Americans.

Archer sucked in a breath through his nose and felt grit in his eyes. The American squad were facing them, guns raised. Compared to his own team, these guys were the stereotypical private contractors in a company uniform of desert boots, sand khakis and navy blue polos, all with fingerless gloves, baseball caps and wrap around shades. Their armour vests were loaded with radios, spare mags and bulging pouches.

Archer recognised them straight away as Black Star operators. Known on the circuit as Death Star due to the high number of lives they both lost and took, they had a terrible reputation for questionable contacts. A couple of their guys were awaiting trial for wiping out an unarmed family in Fallujah the previous year. They were the last guys he wanted to tangle with when everyone was already hot under the collar.

He knew for a fact that many of their guys were either shell shocked vets who should never have been trusted with a gun again, or former soldiers who had been dishonourably discharged. Drug use was apparently rife among their ranks and allegations of looting had been made.

'We're private security,' he told the team leader, 'we've got clients on board and got hit by a couple of IEDs. We've got one KIA and a casualty on board; we could do with a medic.'

His gaze shifted to the gunner who'd shot Bula, standing aside rubbing his throat and eyeing Grunter resentfully.

'Now we've got two KIAs, thanks to you.'

'Ahh thought he's a Taleban,' the guy whined to his commander. 'All them rag heads look the same, sarge.'

'He's Fijian, you fucken Dixie inbreed,' Jacko growled, his nostrils flaring.

The gunner also flared, and stepped forward.

'Who you callin' inbreed, boy?'

'Sergeant, call him off,' Archer warned, deliberately using the team leader's previous rank. He put a hand on Jacko's arm. 'Leave it Jacko.'

'Private!'

'I ain't no Dixie...'

They were nearly toe to toe now.

'Sergeant, control your man,' Archer said forcefully, taking a step forward.

Jacko's fist flashed out and flattened the young gunner's nose across his face, and Archer moved between them, pushing them both back. He turned, holding Jacko back, just in time to catch a jab from the gunner in the side of his face.

He shook it off, opened his mouth to speak again, and took another jab.

Enough's enough.

His own right uppercut came up full force and collected the Black Star gunman under his jaw, lifting him onto his toes and knocking him backwards with his eyes rolling back in his head.

A rifle butt smashed into the side of Archer's skull and everything went black.

MESSAGE FROM THE AUTHOR

Thanks for taking the time to read *Getting Home*. I hope you enjoyed the second book in the **Early Warning** series. The third book in the series is *Stand Fast* - Less than a week after martial law is declared, the country is falling apart. Crime is rampant, led by the brutal Bandits biker gang. And breaking a thousand prisoners out of jail is just the start of their reign of terror...

I'd love it if you could please take the time to leave an online review of *Martial Law* with your favourite book retailer.

If you'd like to know about new releases and receive a free book, sign up to my **Hitlist** on Facebook -

https://www.facebook.com/writer-angus-mclean

Cheers,
Angus McLean

ACKNOWLEDGMENTS

The author would like to thank the advisers who have assisted with the writing of this book. They must remain anonymous for security reasons, but they (and only they) know who they are.

They are the true heroes who put their lives on the line to protect our freedoms. My sincerest gratitude goes out to them.

And once again, huge thanks to "Tori" who does my covers and provides great advice. You rock.

This is a work of fiction, and all errors are the responsibility of the author.

ABOUT THE AUTHOR

Angus McLean is a South Auckland Police officer.

His experience as a cop and a private investigator give his writing a touch of realism. He believes reading should be escapist entertainment and is inspired by the TV shows he watched as a youngster.

His real identity remains a secret.

www.writerangusmclean.com